SUNFLOWERS AND SURRENDER

LM FOX

Editor: Kelly Allenby, Readers Together

Formatter: Bearded Goat Books

Photographer: Wander Aguiar

Graphic Artists: Sarah Paige, The Book Cover Boutique (Ebook) Kate Decided to Design (Paperback)

Models: Kyle K and Sophie

To the Cygnets:
I'm honored to be among you and
incredibly grateful for your endless friendship and support.

Ask, believe, receive, and be immensely thankful
for all is possible
when we live in gratitude and joy.

PLAYLIST

I Found, Amber Run
Move Along, The All-American Rejects
like that, Bea Miller
Walk, Kwabs
Danza Kuduro (featuring Lucenzo), Don Omar
Waka Waka (This Time for Africa), Shakira
Wild Ones (featuring Sia), Flo Rida
FRIENDS, Marshmello & Anne-Marie
Pump Up the Jam, Too House to Handle
Good To Be Alive (Hallelujah), Andy Grammer
THATS WHAT I WANT, Lil Naz X
Don't Start Now, Dua Lipa
Hot n Cold, Katy Perry
Rumor, Lee Brice
If Our Love Is Wrong, Calum Scott
Side to Side (featuring Nicki Minaj), Ariana Grande
Love Someone, Lukas Graham
Nothing Else Matters, Metallica
THE LONELIEST, Maneskin

PLAYLIST

Unstoppable, Sia
Just The Way You Are (featuring Lupe Fiasco),
Bruno Mars

Chapter 1

"Good morning. Thank you for calling Cygnature Blooms, where bigger is always better. You're speaking to Tee, your international representative. We specialize in healing broken hearts worldwide. May I have your location, please?"

"Hi, Tee. I'm calling from Hanover, Virginia."

"Thank you, sir. Please hold while I transfer your call to your local Cygnature Blooms florist."

Tuesday

"Cygnature Blooms, Hanover Square, this is Tuesday. How can I help you today?"

"Hi, Tuesday. I hope you can help me. I need an apology bouquet. Do you think you can assist me?"

"Certainly. I'd be happy to. Is it okay if I ask a few questions to get you the perfect arrangement?"

A nervous chuckle crosses the line as I tap my lower lip with my pen, my mind racing with thoughts of the perfect floral bouquet for such an occasion. Had he snapped at his secretary? Perhaps he forgot his anniversary or his mother's birthday? I begin to flip through the circular file I've created for circumstances like this. If he's more traditional, we could go with roses. But I'm secretly hoping he'll let me use anemones.

"Can I be blunt, Tuesday?"

"Yes, of course. I'm here to help."

"I royally fucked up, and I need to make a grand gesture if I stand a chance in hell of getting my girlfriend to forgive me."

"Oh, gosh. I'm sorry to hear that." *Gah. Now I'm dying to know what happened.* Yet, I can't push for more and remain professional. "Well, I'm sure we can come up with something worthy of whatever may have transpired."

"I doubt that," he mutters. "But that's not your fault. It might take enough flowers to supply the Rose Bowl Parade to get her to forgive me for this."

I remain quiet in case he decides to divulge more. Yet, the line becomes so still I have to question whether the call has disconnected.

"Is your girlfriend located in the Hanover delivery area?" I ask.

"Yes. We live together. That is, I think we still do."

Oh, my. This does sound bad. Deciding to gather his contact information in order to change the subject momentarily, I press on. "Do you mind if I jot down your name and number in case we get disconnected or I need to contact you about delivery details?"

"Sure. My name is Ben. Ben Banks." He rattles off his address and phone number as I enter his details into the computer.

"Well, Ben. I think we can come up with something. Don't lose hope." I refocus on the little wheel of laminated cards I created to help me recall the meanings of various

2

flowers long ago. They've served me well in times like these, helping to determine the right sentiment, season, and color palate the client prefers. *I can't say I've gotten a request quite like this before.* But then again, I'm only a part-time employee here. I'm sure many customers order floral deliveries, hoping it will grant them mercy, yet choose to keep their reasons to themselves.

"There are several flowers that are known to symbolize regret or sadness over a situation. Purple hyacinth, asphodel, white poppy, and scarlet geranium are each known to express consolation. And they are all stunning flowers."

"I think I might need all of them." A heavy exhale followed by a sound akin to the rustling of papers comes from the other end of the line, and I can't help but picture an attractive businessman wearing a shiny, expensive watch as he shuffles papers about his desk. "Tuesday?"

"Yes, sir?"

"Those sound beautiful. But I need over the top." Pause. "My girlfriend means the world to me. I… well, I love her. I didn't realize it until..." Another heavy breath. "Well, until she left me."

My hand instantly flies to my chest as if I'm personally invested in this couple instead of listening to some stranger spill the tea as if I'm a bartender at his favorite saloon. But I don't really understand.

Why is he giving her apology flowers if she left him?

"After dating for several months, she decided she didn't want to be in a committed relationship anymore. She said she was focused on her career and didn't want to have any distractions. But by this time, I was hooked. I wasn't going to beg her to stay. I had my pride. So I let her walk away." Ben grows quiet. When he resumes speaking, his voice cracks a little. "It tore me up more than I expected. Thankfully, it didn't last long, and she came back. But…"

Biting my lip, I anxiously wait for him to continue. While the story is scintillating, it's definitely not relatable. At twenty, I've never had a serious long-term relationship. Sure, I've dated. Yet, regardless of how well the first meeting goes, any chemistry present appears to fizzle by the third. At times, I can't help but question if the lack of attraction is my doing or if my overprotective brother has something to do with it.

My mother often declares how happy she is that I'm a late bloomer with my head in the clouds instead of focused on a boy. She'd prefer I keep my eyes trained on my coursework. Truth be told, she's more committed to my academia and having a career in medicine than I am. I'd much rather spend all of my days working in this little flower shop than continuing college classes toward a nursing degree I have little interest in. Yet, what she doesn't know... there *is* a boy. Well, a man, now. Luckily for her, he's a man who'd never give me a second glance.

"I was upset," Ben continues, interrupting my thoughts. "I felt rejected and drowned my sorrows. A lot. And one of those nights, the alcohol made me weak." I note a longer pause this time and brace myself. "And I hooked up with someone."

Oh, no. Where is this going?

"And apparently, I caught something from them because my girl stormed into my office and practically beat the shit out of me after she received a call from her doctor."

Yikes. Well, at least she's not pregnant. "Oh, Ben."

"Yeah." He sounds so defeated.

Not to sound like Ross and Rachel from Friends, *but they were on a break.*

"I'm hoping she'll forgive me. I mean, *she* left *me*. It was a mistake, but I was drunk and heartbroken. I need to do something to show her how much she means to me."

"Hmm. You're right. This might take more than just flowers." I turn to see the various add-ons we offer when my gaze lands on a few colorful balloons and stuffed animals that I quickly dismiss. "I'm not sure you should focus on forgiveness, Ben. Technically, you didn't do anything wrong." *Well, except maybe the decision to forego using a condom.* I can't help but grimace. "Instead, use this opportunity to demonstrate how much she means to you."

The line grows quiet again. "What do you mean?"

"Like, up your game. You said you love her. Show her. Use this occasion to make this a regular thing. Start by delivering a beautiful assortment of flowers to work, then bring a pretty bouquet of purple hyacinths home a while later. Make her dinner and have them waiting on the table. The following week, greet her with some white poppies and lilacs as you take her to a new restaurant. Run her a bath with rose petals and relaxing essential oils. Let her find chocolates and a love letter. Push yourself farther than you have before in the romance department. Show her your actions are more than asking for forgiveness. It's because you love her."

"You know, you're right. I like that."

"And if she chooses to stay focused on what you did while the two of you were apart rather than what you're doing to bring the two of you together, you can walk away knowing you did all you could." The tinkling metal chime of the bells above the front door steals my attention away from the phone, and as I look up, my heart practically stops beating.

"You're fantastic, Tuesday. Tuesday. Such a pretty name."

"Ben."

"Yes?"

"Keep focused on your girl. I'm going to work on a few ideas and call you back to confirm. Does that sound okay?"

"Yes. Perfect. Thank you. I'm feeling more optimistic already."

"Good. I'm so glad I could help." I disconnect the call, with my eyes still fixated on the only other person in the shop. Despite all of the plants in the showroom doing their part in photosynthesis, I may need to be revived. He's stealing all of the oxygen from the room. This glorious man stands at six foot two with dark brown eyes and wavy brown hair with a single dimple smirking at me. It's enough to make any girl swoon.

"Tues," the deep tone of his familiar voice coats my skin in delectable warmth as it floats in my direction. I feel like a peace lily thriving under a heat lamp. I'm practically melting under his gaze until the front doorbell dings again, and a tall, leggy blonde strolls in, draping her arm through his.

Chapter 2

Tuesday

"Hi, Alex. Ainsley," I add, my tone turning curt with her arrival into my peaceful space. "What brings you to Cygnature Blooms?"

"I wanted to drop this key by for you."

My brows jump in question as he places the shiny metal key into my palm. I turn it about in my hand, enjoying the warmth, unsure if he's been holding it awhile or if it's from the current transferred from his body to mine. "Why are you giving me this?"

"Your brother is going to be away. He has a few different med school interviews over the next week and said you had exams coming and might want to use his place to study."

While I appreciate the sentiment, I'm not sure I understand. "Yeah. I might take him up on it. But I have a key."

Alex looks surprised by this admission. "Did you ever come by when I was living there?"

"Of course not. I wouldn't let myself in uninvited. I only used it when you two were away. Just to have a girls' weekend or some time away from the folks." Still living with my parents at twenty wasn't my preference. Yet it's saving me money, and I'm not home much anyway.

Up until a few months ago, Alex and my brother, Ricky, had been roommates. Once Alex joined the Hanover fire department, he found his own place. He said he was being proactive, preparing for Ricky's departure once he went to medical school. Yet I secretly wonder if he had difficulty sleeping after his twenty-four-hour shifts with Ricky's girlfriend spending more time at their place.

"Why don't you keep this? I have one. Who knows. You might need it for something one day," I say.

"Man." Ainsley huffs. "And here I got excited thinking you brought me here to get me something pretty."

My eyes flick to Alex, who looks as if he's trying hard to prevent an eye roll. I'd wonder what he sees in her, but anyone with eyes can answer that question. She's tall and thin with long blonde hair and blue eyes. She's one of the popular girls from the rescue squad I volunteer with. Ainsley is so self-absorbed that it'd take more than her looks if *I* was a man, but I'm starting to think they can easily look past that if the packaging is appealing.

Yet, I didn't think Alex was like the other men my brother's age. And certainly not like the boys I know. Sure, he dates plenty of girls, but he seems more mature. But I admit I probably see him through rose-colored glasses.

My brother met Alex while volunteering with the rescue squad five years ago. While Ricky was focused on medical school, Alex had always dreamt of joining the fire department. In the beginning, he was just my brother's hot new friend. But the more time he spent with our family, the harder I fell. He's nearly five years older than I am. I'm well aware that's a lifetime when one of you is an adult, drinking and living on your own, while even though I'm twenty, I still look too young to attempt using a fake I.D. and live with my parents.

I've felt like I've lived under lock and key my whole life. I blame the fact that I'm the youngest on why my parents seem to be the helicopter variety—always hovering over-head, monitoring every facet of my life. The same doesn't seem to be true for my brother. Yet, Thomas Richard Palmer was born a near clone of my parents. He played with their doctors' instruments at home as a child, professing to follow in their footsteps. I, on the other hand, preferred to play in the dirt.

My mom and dad, an internist and a surgeon, respectively, remain driven to keep medicine at the forefront of my career plans. A family of medical providers. I'm unsure if my unimpressive grades, the absence of drive toward competing for medical school acceptance, or my lack of enthusiasm over their interesting cases have made them wary of my ability to continue the family career tree. But so far, they haven't backed down.

The door chimes again, bringing my focus to the front of the shop. My wild and wonderful friend, Grace, strolls in carrying a bag of take-out from our favorite bistro, and I can almost feel my stomach start to grumble. She walks behind the counter as if she owns the place, and I don't miss the scornful sneer in Ainsley's direction.

"Okay, we're heading out. Catch you later, Sunny T." Alex's deep chocolate orbs and flirty dimple throw one more log on this internal flame burning bright for him.

"Bye, Alex. Ainsley." I try a little harder not to say her name with complete disdain. It's not her fault that I wish he were mine. She may be pretty, but she's a superficial leech. He has to know she's made her way through half of the men at the rescue squad and the fire department before she latched onto him. *I guess the police department is next.*

"Sunny T?" Grace interrupts my thoughts.

"Yeah. Alex is the king of nicknames. My brother went by his given name, Thomas, until Alex came along. But he started calling him T Ricky, and it stuck. Now even my parents call him Ricky." I laugh.

"So, where did Sunny T come from?"

"I don't know for certain. But I'm assuming Ricky told him about how I used to drink Sunny Delight all the time as a kid."

"The orange drink?"

"Yeah."

"What's he call Ainsley?" She shakes her head in disgust. "Never mind. I really don't want to know."

"You know, I don't remember him ever using anything but her real name." *Hmm. Seems odd now that I think about it.*

"I think Airhead fits," Grace adds. Snickering in her direction, I take in my gorgeous friend. Graceland Montgomery is a five-foot-six stunner named for her mother's love of all things Elvis. She's a natural beauty. Her porcelain skin is flawless, set against perfect bright white teeth and shining blue eyes framed by naturally long dark lashes. Yet she seems utterly unaware of how attractive she is. Instead of playing up her features in figure-hugging attire, she gravitates toward boho chick. Oversized floral is her jam.

Retrieving a soup container from the take-out bag, she continues, "So why on earth were they here?"

"Oh, Ricky has started traveling to medical schools for interviews. Alex brought by a key to his place in case I wanted a reprieve from the parentals."

Grace's eyes brighten, and she dances in place. "Oh." She claps. "While the mouse is away, the cat will play."

Chapter 3

Tuesday

"Oh. No more," I tell Grace, pushing away the tray of sushi. "It's so good. I could eat all of them by myself."

"Don't do that. You won't have room for ice cream later."

"All of us can't eat whatever we want and maintain a perfect figure like you." I give her a playful jab. I take in the coffee table in Ricky's apartment and chuckle. "We're pathetic. Most twenty-year-olds who managed a girls' weekend in their brother's apartment would be treating themselves to drinks and painting each other's nails. We're doing homework, eating vegetables, and watching *Pride and Prejudice* for about the one-hundredth time."

"Okay, don't mock it. It's the best movie ever made," Grace declares, lifting her hand and awaiting my high-five. "Besides. We're mature, responsible girls. If we want to go to that squad party at Vincent's house on Saturday night, we better knock out the homework now. 'Cause Sunday, we're going to be useless."

This is where the 'mice will play,' as Grace so eloquently put it.

My life at the rescue squad is more akin to the blue-haired volunteers who man the phones than the rest of the EMTs. While constant parties are happening, it's pointless attending one if my brother is within a sixty-mile radius. I'd be forced into a corner, like being assigned to the children's table at a holiday function. Watched, guarded, and practically branded as if wearing an "off limits" sign around my neck.

Grace understands the dilemma. She's seen Ricky's domineering behavior when we've been out with him and his girlfriend, Julia. I've given up pushing back against it. He's the self-appointed family bodyguard against men 'on the prowl.' But we're young and deserve the chance to have fun and meet someone attractive.

"So, what are we wearing tomorrow night?" I admit this line of questioning may be to ensure she doesn't have some new thrift store find she's dying to try out. I don't want us to stand out. The whole point of going to these parties is to have fun, blend in, and enjoy this time of my life.

"Don't worry, T. I'm just wearing jeans and a T-shirt." She laughs. "The real question is, what are *you* wearing?" She waggles her brows at me. We both know we're hoping we can attract some handsome, eligible mates, preferably with date potential. But, honestly, I'd settle for one evening of feeling admired.

"Something to show off my assets." I giggle, stretching my sleep shirt tight against my breasts. They're a C cup, one of my best features, and I admit I'm not ashamed to flaunt them.

Okay, when Ricky's away.

WE ARRIVE AT THE PARTY IN FULL SWING. VINCENT'S HOUSE reminds me of something you'd see on Greek Row. But it's in the burbs. The house is shared with three roommates, and the yard and interior look every bit the frat house. As we cross the threshold, the stench of stale beer hits me in the face, and there's a sticky sensation beneath my shoes when I walk.

Leaning into Grace, I ask, "Remind me why we've been dying to go to one of these again."

"Think of it as a rite of passage." She laughs. "And if that doesn't do it for ya, then think of it as a department store. You just need to try on a few men and see which one fits."

"Oh, lord." I giggle.

We make our way toward the kitchen and attempt to locate a drink that appears safe. I haven't acquired a taste for beer, so the keg is out. We agree to avoid anything that's already open or strong enough to cloud our judgment. I don't need to hear any 'I told you so's' from Ricky once he returns.

"Score!" Grace squeals. My eyes flick to her and find her holding two wine coolers that she's retrieved from the back of the fridge. Popping the caps with ease, she hands me one, and we quickly clink our bottles. Looking down at the beverage, it appears to be some overly fruity concoction. But it sure beats beer.

Grace does the same and shrugs her shoulders. "Let's get pineappled." We both laugh.

Moving into the other room, I grab ahold of the back of Grace's shirt in an effort not to get separated. It's a lot more crowded than I expected. Occasionally we stop to greet the faces we recognize but continue pushing through the sea of warm bodies until we can reach the other side of the room.

"Whew. That was a workout," Grace yells over the heavy base pounding under our feet. We both nurse our drinks, pointing at various people we recognize and questioning who their dance partners might be.

"Hey, Tuesday. Fancy seeing you here. I didn't think you ever came to these."

Trying to think fast, I respond, "I do. Sometimes it's so crowded I probably just blend in." I can practically feel Grace's chuckle tickle my side at my absurd statement. *As if.*

Xane gives me a deliberate once-over, letting his eyes roam from my head to my toes. "I doubt you could ever blend, babe." He drags his tongue across his lower lip, and my heart rate picks up. I wasn't expecting anything like this to happen so quickly. All right, let's be real. I wasn't expecting anything like this to happen *at all.*

"I'm going to go back for a few more drinks," Grace says, nudging me with her elbow. Lifting my bottle, I'm shocked I finished mine so quickly. I guess I wasn't nursing this after all. Nerves probably.

"So, you want to dance?" Xane asks.

"Sure."

He takes my hand and leads me a few steps into the crowd before pulling me into him and swaying to the sounds of Flo Rida singing "Wild Ones." Xane is cute. He's got sandy blond hair that gives him a surfer vibe. I'm not clueless about his exploits. He's been paired with many girls in this room. But I'm only dancing with him.

What's the harm in that?

Chapter 4

Alex

What the fuck is she up to?

I should've known the minute Ricky's back was turned, his sweet, innocent little sister would get herself in over her head. This party is no place for a girl like her.

"I'm going to grab some drinks," Ainsley says.

Looking over my shoulder as she heads toward the kitchen, I shake my head. She's wearing a skin-tight dark gray dress that barely covers her ass. Why on earth did she wear that? The only reason this doesn't irritate me as much as seeing Tuesday here is that I'm well aware of how many people have already seen Ainsley's ass.

Ainsley is a cute girl. And she's always up for a good time. It's all I was interested in when we got together. I hadn't planned on this turning into a relationship. But she sunk her claws in and hasn't let go. I figured she'd eventually move on or get too clingy, opening the door to telling her I wasn't interested in more. But so far, it's tolerable. And ultimately, it distracts me from who I really want but can't have.

My gaze falls on Tuesday, dancing with that asshole, Xane. What does she see in that loser? He's your typical playboy, collecting notches on his bedpost for every girl he lays, most of which are squad members. She can do a lot better than him.

Tuesday is a timeless beauty. She's tall and, while fit, has curves in all the right places. She has long, auburn hair, fair skin dotted with a few freckles across her nose and cheeks, and the most stunning green eyes I've ever seen. I know she's dated a few boys through the years, but I can't recall a long-term steady boyfriend.

Hell. Is she a virgin? Fuck. I can't let my mind go there.

My blood begins to boil as I watch her run her fingers through Xane's hair as they dance entirely too close. She finally takes a step away as Grace approaches with another clear bottle of something that doesn't look like soda. *How many has she had?*

She's not dressed for a nightclub like Ainsley, but instead, she's wearing a thin cotton top that caresses her tits in a way I don't think I've noticed before. *And trust me, I've noticed.* One sleeve is draped precariously down her shoulder, exposing her bra's thin black strap and creamy skin. My fingers tingle with the desire to stroke her soft flesh before returning her shirt where it belongs.

But that ass. It's as if her jeans were painted onto her delicious perky backside. It's the stuff dreams are made of. And what's more, I'm sure she has no idea how alluring she is. Unlike Ainsley, who constantly treats her appearance like a tryout for a reality show, Tuesday remains blissfully unaware. If she is, she certainly doesn't let it show.

Xane's hands drop down to grip the curvy globes of

her ass, and I see red. Pulling out my phone, I decide to let her know that while her brother is away, I've reported for duty.

Alex

10:20 p.m.
Alex: What do you think you're doing?
As if on cue, Tuesday reaches behind her and retrieves her phone from her back pocket. Her head quickly rotates from side to side as she attempts to pinpoint my location.
10:24 p.m.
Sunny T: I'm dancing.

10:28 P.M.
Alex: That's not dancing. If he was any closer, he'd be inside you.

10:29 P.M.
Alex: Back away from the asshole, T!
I can almost feel her exasperated groan reverberate from across the room and expect her to step back, only to see her slide her phone into her back pocket and accept a drink from the fucktard. An open drink in a solo cup, no less. She knows better than that. She must've had too many already.

Making my way to where they're standing because that's sure as hell not dancing, I'm interrupted by Ainsley and some random chick she's brought with her.

"Alex, babe, this is Cassandra. She wanted to meet you," Ainsley says, already sounding a little tipsy. How long have I been standing here glowering at Tues?

"Hey," I greet, not bothering to make eye contact. I'm not letting Tuesday out of my sight. Instant relief washes over me when I watch her hand off her red solo cup to Grace. She gives Tuesday a knowing glance, and I thank God her friend is looking out for her. This should have me feeling more relaxed, except Xane's fucking hands are back on her ass. While I appreciate Grace's help, looking out for Tuesday is clearly a two-person job.

"Babe. Dance with us," Ainsley whines.

Us? Normally, the thought of being sandwiched between two women would sound appealing. But if Ainsley is offering, it's purely for attention. What's more, I have a Defcon three situation happening over here.

"Not right now, Ainsley." I grab my phone, planning to send a final message to Tuesday before physically removing Xane's body from hers. Using the text as an excuse, I tell Ainsley, "I was supposed to message Ricky earlier and forgot."

"Fine." She pouts. "We'll just find someone else to dance with."

I'm tempted to thank Ainsley for her petty threat, but I don't want to antagonize her. My eyes drift back to Tuesday just in time to see Xane squat down, then grind his body into hers on his ascent.

For fuck's sake.

10:40 P.M.

Alex: *Last chance, or you'll have his murder on your hands.*

Standing with my legs spread and arms crossed over my chest in a determined stance, I wait. And wait. She suddenly throws her head back in laughter, her dark cinnamon tresses spilling down her back just as that dickhead leans forward and places his fucking mouth on her neck.

That's it!

Storming over to where they're standing, I don't even try to hide my ire. I see Grace take a step back out of the corner of my eye.

"I think we're done here."

Chapter 5

Alex

I don't even have to acknowledge Xane. He's well aware of Ricky's stance on anyone messing with his sister. Grabbing her arm, I pull her toward where Grace is standing, and the smell of wine cooler hits me in the face. Gone is the sweet smell of flowers and innocence. It didn't take much to snow this lightweight.

"You're drunk."

"So."

"So? What the hell would've happened if I hadn't been here."

"I probably would've had a good time." She huffs.

"Grace, I'm taking her home before she gets into any more trouble. Do you need a ride?"

"No, I drove us. Sorry, Alex. We just wanted to have some fun. I didn't realize she could get this tipsy off of a few wine coolers."

"Well, the only one who would've bragged about his 'fun' to everyone would've been Xane. No telling what he would've done to you, with or without your consent, before he plastered pictures of you all over social media. It would've been your word against his. That guy's a dick."

Both Grace and Tuesday appear to sober up a fraction at this, but I'm not taking any chances. "I'm letting Ainsley know she needs to find a ride or come with us. Please be careful, Grace. Most of these guys aren't respectable."

"I won't stay much longer. Thank you for taking care of her, Alex."

"Her?" Hiccup. "I'm standing right here." Hiccup.

Grace comes in for a hug and whispers something into Tuesday's ear I can't hear. They both giggle before Grace turns on her heel, and I lead Tuesday in search of Ainsley.

"Ains," I yell, spotting her sitting on top of the dining table holding court. She has several men around her, all jockeying for her attention. "I've got to take Tuesday home. You coming?"

"What? No. We just got here."

"Can you get a ride home? I can't stay." This is a dumb question. I'm sure any one of these guys will offer. *I might have to double up on condoms with her from here on out or break it off with Ainsley once and for all. I don't trust her farther than I can throw her.*

She gives me a deadpan look as if to mock me.

"Okay, be safe. I'll talk to you tomorrow."

As I turn toward the door, I notice Tuesday wiggling her fingers at Ainsley as if to taunt her, and I immediately grab her hand, tucking it into my side. The last thing this evening needs is Ainsley having suspicions about my best friend's little sister. Not only is Ainsley the center of attention at most of these events, but she has no problem stirring up shit if it'll bring her more of the same.

I lift my wobbly companion and place her in the front seat of my truck. As I lean over to buckle her in, I feel her nose nuzzling my hair. I should be annoyed at her antics tonight, but I have to tamp down my smile.

I've had my suspicions that this freckle-faced beauty might be attracted to me. Initially, it was awkward. The nearly five-year age gap may not be a big deal now, but when she was underage, it was somewhat jarring. But as she grew older, I couldn't ignore the way I felt constantly drawn to her. Yet I knew then, just as I do now, this girl would be forever off-limits given my friendship with her brother... so, there's no sense letting my mind go there.

T Ricky and I have been tight since the day we met. His friendship means everything to me. Truthfully, I'm already mourning the loss of him. Four years of medical school is a long time. Even if he attended college closer to home, spending time with him might be too distracting. His studies will likely eat up all of his time. Hell, he even asked his girlfriend to keep a long-distance relationship because her moving with him would be too difficult for the first few years.

I know how protective he is of Tuesday. I haven't been a dirty sleazebag like Xane, but I've enjoyed my youth, and there's been no lack of women. I'm sure he's picturing someone more honorable than me to eventually date his sister. Plus, if I did go out with her and it didn't work out... I don't want to think what would become of me once I lost their whole family. Because there's no doubt that's what would happen if I hurt her.

Giggling from the passenger seat startles me back to the present as I turn the engine and head for Ricky's place. There's no way I can take her to her parents like this.

"Alex. Alexander. Alexander Bell." Another giggle, this

one ending on a snort. "Is your middle name Graham?" She teases.

I keep my eyes on the road, trying to ignore her until we get to Ricky's place.

Her soft hand lands on my forearm, and a jolt of electricity shoots straight to my core. "Is it?" Her body is now twisted in my direction, with her hands steepled together as if she's begging me to answer. God, she's cute. Even when she's drunk.

"My first name is."

Her mouth immediately falls open, and she begins to cackle, rolling to and fro within the confines of her seatbelt.

"It's not that funny. It's a family name."

"Ahoy there!" She snorts.

"Oh My God. What are you babbling about? We're in a car, not a boat, you sauced little sunflower."

More laughter erupts from her. "No. I remember doing a school project on Alexander Graham Bell once." Hiccup. "He wanted people to answer the phone and say, "Ahoy there." She giggles. "It was Thomas Edison who told everyone to say hello." She snorts.

"Thanks for the lesson, you maniac. Are you trying out for that show, *Drunk History*?" I chuckle. "Now keep it together until we get to Ricky's place. I don't want memories of this evening spewed all over my truck."

I arrive at the apartment complex, gather her out of the truck, and lead her upstairs. Luckily, the apartment is on the second floor because I'm tempted to carry her at the rate we're going with these steps. We no sooner make it inside than I lead her to the bathroom and encourage her to do whatever she needs to get herself ready for bed. While she's taking a leak or brushing her teeth, I find a glass and fill it with cool water, retrieve the Ibuprofen from the pantry, and grab the kitchen trash can to bring to the bedroom in case these wine coolers come back to haunt her.

After ten minutes of near silence, I get nervous that she's passed out and knock on the door. "Sunny? You okay?"

"Hmm."

"T, what's up? Come on out so you can sleep this off." Still nothing. I crack the door, peeking in to ensure she's not completely naked, and find her sitting on the side of the tub. Coming closer, I lower my voice a bit. "What're you doing, T?" As sheltered as her family keeps her, I have to remind myself this girl has probably not had many chances to drink.

"I can't get my pants off."

Well fuck. "Do you need to go to the bathroom?"

She shakes her head, her hair falling like a curtain around her face.

"Come on, Sunny. Let's get you into bed."

Her facial expression is almost comical as she gazes up at me with a doe-eyed expression.

"Are you going to remember any of this tomorrow?" I chuckle. "Up and at 'em, you little temptress." I wrap an arm around her and encourage her toward the guest room. My old room.

Once I sit her down on the edge of the bed, I watch as she attempts to wriggle out of her skinny jeans and try not to laugh out loud. Grabbing ahold of the waistband, I carefully pull them down her legs. My hands start to tremble, and I scold myself as my cock jumps in my pants. Sitting on the floor as her feet dangle over the edge of the bed, I remove one foot and then the other. Her skin is silky smooth, and I'm dying to lean forward and drag my tongue along the inside of her thighs.

As I unfurl her pants and stand to lay them on the end of the bed, I nearly come undone. She's managed to remove one arm from her shirt while I was wrestling with her pants. Her breasts taunt me from the lacy black bra she's wearing. The delicate material is in contrast to the little white boy shorts she has on that are doing a number on my dick.

"Whoa, whoa, whoa. What are you doing?"

Chapter 6

Alex

"Getting ready for bed," she answers matter-of-factly, still wriggling in her shirt.

"What? You sleep in the buff? Never mind. Don't answer that." *I don't want to know. I'll never get that vision out of my head.*

"I don't sleep naked. But I don't want to sleep in my bra."

Fuck. And now I'm thinking about her tits.

"And my shirt smells like old beer."

"Were you mixing beer and fruity drinks?" No wonder she's a mess.

"No. Xane spilled it on me."

Fucker.

"He offered to lick it off." She laughs.

"I suggest you stop talking, or you'll have to put yourself to sleep with one arm stuck in your shirt because I'm going to be busy ripping that asshole's tongue from his face."

A mixture of a giggle and hiccup escapes, and I quickly reach for the trashcan.

"Are you going to be sick?"

"Nope," she says, still squirming inside her top.

I place the trashcan down and head for the closet, where some of my T-shirts remain. Returning to Tuesday's side, I sit her up so her back is to my chest and help to free her remaining arm. "Sunny, slide your bra straps down. I'm going to slide this shirt over your head, and we can get your bra off after you're covered." Hell. The mere notion of taking her bra off, covered or not, has gotten me to full mast.

"Okay." Her minty breath dances over my face.

Once Tuesday is settled, I pull back the sheets and scoot her into bed. "You sure you don't feel sick?"

"Nope." Hiccup. As her breaths get heavier, I grow wary about leaving her. What if she throws up during the night? She's barely taking up any space in this queen-sized bed, so I slide in before I can contemplate what I'm doing.

Chapter 7

Tuesday

My eyes blink open, the view between the narrow slits blurry and unfocused. I try to push through the fog to connect with my surroundings but wonder if I'm too distracted by the sandpaper currently residing where my tongue should be. Eventually, the haze clears, and I notice there's an arm draped around me.

What the heck?

I immediately sort through the cloudy memories from last night. My lids spring wide, and I slowly trail my gaze from the muscular hand up the chorded forearm, up, up, up until I find the familiar sharp jawline of Alexander Bell. My body jolts within his arms, the slight movement causing me to shift against something very hard, poking into my back.

Holy hell.

My mind is reeling. What happened? My eyes snap

shut, and I attempt to push further, chasing the images of the last thing I remember.

Those texts last night.

Alex was hot that I was dancing with Xane. But the time between then and now is a mystery. As much as I love the feeling of being wrapped up in his arms, I quickly twist in his solid embrace to get answers.

Did we? Holy crap, did we have sex, and I missed the whole thing?

I start to get teary-eyed about the situation when Alex awakens.

"Did we?"

He blinks momentarily as if trying to escape the same fog I just emerged from. His deep brown orbs become wide with alarm before he blurts, "Fuck no!"

As much as I'm relieved by this, his response has my tears about to tumble down my cheeks for a different reason. I can't hide feeling offended by his defiant remark.

"Your brother would kill me."

This follow-up is too little, too late. Alex Bell couldn't make it any clearer that he has absolutely no interest in me. I'm so stupid. I'm sure there's some logical reason for how we ended up here, me in his T-shirt and no bra, but I'm too hurt to care anymore. Maybe he was drunk and thought I was Ainsley. Whatever the reason, I definitely didn't miss anything good.

I sit up, swiping at my eyes before Alex sees the effect he's had on me. Why couldn't I have laid there and pretended for a few more minutes before confronting him?

Swinging my legs over the edge of the bed, I grab my jeans and top and head for the bathroom. "Thanks for getting me to bed."

Ugh, that didn't come out right. Whatever.

Just get me out of here.

Chapter 8

Tuesday

"Happy birthday," Grace squeals, holding at least a dozen multicolored mylar balloons in the storefront of Cygnature Blooms.

"This feels a little backward. Having them delivered here." I laugh.

"Well, you deserve all of the celebrating you can handle. You don't turn twenty-one every day. Look out, bitches. Time to get your party on!"

My mind instantly harkens to the last time I 'got my party on,' and I wince. "Well, I think I might have a frozen cocktail with dinner and call it a night."

The memory of that night remains foggy. Add to it the painful morning after. Heck, I didn't even have sex and still had to do the walk of shame. I bolted out of there like my hair was on fire. Alex tried to take me home, but I didn't want to be near him after his declaration. *"Fuck no!"* Those two little words still haunt me.

"Uh, Tuesday?" Nolan interrupts from the back of the shop.

"Oh, hey. What's up?"

"So, I have some deliveries."

Is Nolan having a stroke? He's only a few years older than me, so that seems unlikely. But isn't it his sole job to make deliveries?

"Okay. Thanks for letting me know." I look at Grace and shrug my shoulders in confusion.

"No. They're for you." He chuckles. They came in this morning while you were in class. Jo Jo put the orders together and left them next to my other deliveries with a note saying they were to be delivered to you."

"Oh, wow. Okay." My cheeks flush in anticipation. I'm never on the receiving end of these.

Nolan darts back into the back of the shop and emerges with two large bouquets. One has an assortment of colorful fall flowers. I reach for the card and read the message.

Happy birthday. Love, Ricky

Awe. That's so sweet. I'm meeting him and my parents for dinner. I'm surprised he wouldn't have just given me my gift then. But they're beautiful. Burying my nose into the bouquet, I take a deep inhale of the fragrant blossoms. He knows how much I love flowers. They're the perfect gift.

Nolan extends the remaining vase containing a dozen large, bold sunflowers, and my heart skips a beat. They've always been my favorite. With my birthday in November, it's always felt like they're my birthday flower. Alas, it's really the chrysanthemum. Yet sunflowers bring such joy when I look at them. To birds also, apparently, given they attract butterflies, hummingbirds, and the like to their nectar. What's more, it's thought they symbolize loyalty and adoration. Two qualities I admire.

Plucking the small card from the vase, I open the envelope and take in the inscription.

Happy birthday, Sunny T.

I can't think of you without picturing a sunflower tucked behind your ear,

just as you looked the first time I saw you.

Love, Alex

WAIT. WHAT? THAT'S WHERE MY NICKNAME CAME FROM? Tapping my fingernail against my lower lip, I try to remember the first time I saw Alex. I can picture him clear as day, standing beside my brother. They were about to go to the lake together, and I thought he was the most handsome boy I'd ever met. But for the life of me, I couldn't tell you what I looked like.

"They're so pretty," Grace says as she looks over my shoulder.

"They're my favorite. Flower, I mean."

"Well, between his message on that card and the way he was looking at you the other night at the party…"

Spinning on my heel, I startle Grace with my unhinged reaction. "What way he was looking at me? Grace, spill it. I don't remember anything after receiving some texts from him while I was dancing with Xane."

A mischievous smirk lifts the corner of her mouth. "He was hot. And not his usual fuck hot. He was about to lose it when you were touching Xane. But when Xane put his mouth on your neck, he went ballistic. I don't care what anyone says, he's never been that possessive over Ainsley."

As much as I'd love to believe her, I can't help but think

he's just an extension of Ricky. He was only stepping up to protect me as my brother would have. Nothing more.

———

MOM, DAD, AND I WALK INTO LUIGI'S AND ARE GREETED with hugs from the owner. We've been coming to this local Italian Eatery for years. Much like many who live in Hanover, celebrating birthdays, milestones, and achievements is all the more delicious here.

Luigi escorts us to a large table in the center of the room, where we find Ricky, his girlfriend, Julia, and Alex waiting for us. Seeing his handsome face for the first time since running from my brother's apartment feels awkward. But at least he didn't invite Ainsley to my birthday.

We all say hello and settle into our menus to make our choices. This keeps us quiet for a few moments, given there's so much to pick from. I decide on the Penne alla Vodka with a side salad and await the others when Luigi asks if I'd like something from the bar. My eyes immediately dart to meet Alex's, the memory of waking up wrapped in his arms, his firm erection in my back causing my cheeks to warm.

"I don't have a lot of experience with drinks yet. Could I just have a Daquari?"

"Of course! A birthday Daquari coming up. Would you like strawberry?"

"That sounds great, Luigi. Thank you." As he walks away, my gaze bounces back to Alex, whose stare is trained on me. I can't quite make out his expression, but the intensity causes the blush that had just faded to quickly return.

"Did you get the flowers?" Ricky asks. He gives Julia a subtle smile, and I realize the delivery was her doing.

"Oh, yes. I'm so sorry. I loved them. Thank you. And thank you, too, Alex. It was very thoughtful."

Ricky appears taken aback that Alex would've sent me flowers, looking skeptically at his friend before reaching for his water. Alex doesn't say anything. He simply smiles, his eyes so dark and dreamy. Okay, I have to stop looking at him, or everyone here will know something's up.

"Your dad and I wanted to deliver your present in person." My mother slides a card over to where I'm sitting. Typically, my mother uses my birthday as an excuse to shop. I'm grateful for whatever they've gotten me, but it's usually not small enough to fit in a card.

As I carefully tear the envelope to retrieve the contents, I glance up to see everyone watching me closely. I get the distinct impression they all know what lies within.

Happy birthday, honey.

Turning twenty-one can be an exciting time.
We don't want to cramp your style but give you the opportunity to enjoy your newfound freedom. So we're taking you on a three-day cruise out of Miami next weekend.
Bon Voyage!
Love, Mom and Dad

"Oh my gosh! Really? I've always wanted to go on a cruise."

"Yes. Your brother is bringing Julia, and even Alex is coming along."

There go my cheeks again.

———

A WEEK LATER, IT'S CRUISE WEEKEND. THANKFULLY, I didn't have to work. Although the owners of Cygnature Blooms are amazing. I'm certain they would've found a way to make the trip work. The forecast calls for warm weather and sunny skies, which is the perfect juxtaposition to our cool November days of late. I've packed my bright yellow bathing suit into my carry-on bag and plan to wear it under my sunflower sundress the minute I'm onboard. I'm making the most of these three days. I just need to make sure my thoughts aren't drawn to a certain hot fire-fighter the whole time.

Our flight arrived in Miami last night. Mom and Dad didn't want to risk flight delays traveling on the day of embarkation. Apparently, Alex, Ricky, and Julia had no such fear as they were flying in today.

"Anyone heard from Ricky?" I ask my father.

"No. But I checked their flight, and it was on time. Don't worry. I'm sure they'll make it."

It's wall-to-wall people as we proceed through the check-in process at the Miami cruise port terminal. The area is buzzing with excitement in anticipation of the jour-ney. We take a seat, reviewing the pamphlet containing the ship's schedule for our cruise until we're allowed to board. The experience is so new and exciting. I'm certain that's what has my nerves jumping. Not the anticipation of spending three days with—

"There they are," Mom says, sounding relieved.

My head pops up from my leaflet to see Ricky, Julia, Alex... and Ainsley.

Chapter 9

Tuesday

"Oh, I'm so excited about this weekend I can barely stand it," Ainsley squeals from beneath the largest beach hat I've ever seen. She looks like a reality show star from the *Real Housewives* of Suburbia. Her outfit is ridiculous. It's as if she found a life-size Barbie Cruise Line ensemble. All big, bold black and white striped nautical attire paired with black and white wedge heels and that over-the-top spaceship doubling as a sunhat. All while the rest of us are wearing shorts or sundresses.

Ugh. Why did he have to bring her? Normally, I can handle being around him and whomever he's dating. Granted, Ainsley is probably the most annoying of the lot, but I've come to accept my crush is unrequited. Letting myself consider anything else simply because he was kind enough to watch over my drunk self, his body wrapped around me like a python in the bed, is one birthday wish I need to let go of. I'll only end up hurt if I allow myself to keep dreaming of him. Whether it's the age difference, the fact I'm his best friend's little sister, or he simply doesn't think of me in that way, that ship has sailed. It's time to move on.

I'm determined to enjoy this cruise regardless of Alex and Ainsley. It's my birthday. My parents didn't pay for this amazing trip, only for me to hold up in my cabin with a book. Alex can go enjoy his Paris Hilton wannabe. I'm living la vida loca.

My pulse thrums within my chest as the overhead announcement finally advises our turn to board the ship. I grab my mother's arm to calm my nerves. "Thank you for doing this, Mom. I can't think of a better way to celebrate my twenty-first birthday."

"I'm so glad, Tuesday. You work so hard and never give us an ounce of trouble. You deserve this. But don't let the fruity drinks get away from you. I don't want you to spend the whole cruise feeling bad, or worse, puking your guts up."

Been there, done that. Thankfully, minus the puke.

"I'll be careful. I'm glad we decided to have the bags delivered to our room. Once we get onboard, I'm going straight to the pool to change into my suit and soak up the sun."

My mother laughs, patting my hand. "I'm going to grab some lunch but save me a seat by the pool."

TWENTY MINUTES LATER, I'VE CHANGED INTO MY BIKINI but keep my sundress on for now. I've managed to find a row of unoccupied seats and place my backpack and towel down as I observe the area. The deep blue pool is small but inviting. Yet there are plenty of places for guests to stretch out and enjoy the sun's rays.

Having only imagined what cruising would be like, I assumed everything would feel claustrophobic—cramped, confined spaces with throngs of people. But the layout of this ship is quite the opposite. The opulence of the main floor took my breath away as we entered the vessel. And it's clear each new location we enter is designed for maximum functionality as well as aesthetics. This particular ship is geared toward adults with many options for entertainment. While I'm not typically into clubbing and the like, it's my first cruise, so I hope to check out all the options after dinner.

I reach for my bag and retrieve my sunscreen. The last thing I need is to end up with sunburn for the remainder of the trip. I squeeze a small amount into the palms of my hands and dab the cream lightly onto my face, neck, and chest. Festive music plays overhead, adding to the celebratory vibe aboard. The coconut scent of the lotion only enhances the overall atmosphere. Uniformed wait staff meander about the pool deck taking drink orders, and the chaise lounges are filling quickly.

"Hey, T. Will you grab a couple of chairs for me and Julia?" Ricky asks as they follow Mom and Dad toward the buffet for lunch.

"Sure. I'll try. I'm not sure how many I'll be able to get away with." At least we don't have to compete with families with kids spending their days poolside.

"I'll stay and watch a couple," Alex says. "You go on in and eat, Ains. I'm not hungry."

"Okay, babe. If you're sure." Ainsley and the satellite dish sitting atop her head clomp along behind Ricky and Julia as Alex's deep brown eyes land on me. It's like they're trying to say something.

They're saying look away before you fall under their spell, you idiot.

"You need help with that?" Alex asks.

I'm confused about what he's referring to until he dips his chin toward the bottle of sunscreen in my hand. As tempting as this may be, I can't handle his hands on my body only to watch him do the same to Ainsley. "No. I've got it."

The beat of the music seems to change to a Latin dance number, and a few guests make their way toward a makeshift dance floor at the pool's edge in front of the DJ. I decide to use this opportunity to distance myself from the firefighter who is only adding to the heat on this ship right now. "Could you get me a drink, though? Something fun with an umbrella."

"Just don't overdo it, Sunny."

The memory of the message on his sweet birthday card makes my cheeks warm at the nickname. I inadvertently reach up to touch them. "I know, I know. I learned my lesson," I say to Alex's back as he walks away.

I make my way to the group of sail-away partygoers and find a place to get my groove on when a tall, attractive dark-haired male wearing a bright red shirt, white uniform pants, and a nametag approaches and starts to dance with me. It reads Ricardo, Cruise Director.

Well, hello, Ricardo.

ALEX

Wow, that was a little too easy. I pocket the stateroom card given at check-in after charging two drinks to my room and recall a buddy at the fire department warning me how the onboard fees can add up quickly. I need to keep my wits about me in the alcohol, Tuesday, and financial departments.

Strolling to the lounge chairs where I'd left Tuesday moments ago, I have to do a double take to ensure I've located the right seats since she's walked away. Finding her drawstring backpack and sunscreen on her bright towel, I confirm these are ours. I place our drinks on the small metal table between our chairs and casually look about the pool deck as I recline... then freeze.

What the fuck?

My sweet, innocent Sunny T is dirty dancing with some guy that appears to work for the cruise line.

Wait... my Sunny T?

He has his hands on her lower back as they sway their hips back and forth. He's entirely too close for this to be considered a work function. He gives her a salacious grin as he slides his hands to her hips while mine simultaneously ball into fists. If this keeps up, the fire alarms are going to go off from the steam pouring out of my ears before the ship gets a foot from shore.

He twirls her around in circles, her arm extended overhead before he pulls away from her body. I only relax briefly before he crouches in front of her as she spins, fluffing her skirt so it rises high enough to reveal her bright yellow bikini bottom.

Jesus.

I'm torn between ripping her away from him or dancing with her myself when I notice the song changes to a Shakira tune, and he gives her an air kiss before moving to another partygoer. *Thank fuck.*

Tuesday whirls in my direction, her hand over her heart as if she's trying to catch her breath, and any thoughts of scolding her for dancing with Rico Suave disappear as I see her radiant smile. My breath becomes lodged in my throat.

When did my best friend's little sister turn into a beauty queen?

As if it's time for the bathing suit portion of this Miss Universe contest to begin, Tuesday stops beside her chaise lounge, lifts her flouncy sundress, and drops it on her towel. My mouth is like the Sahara as I take in her curves, covered in nothing but this tiny yellow string bikini.

This girl is the very definition of breathtaking. I think I've forgotten to inhale, almost catatonic at the sight of her. The sneak peeks of her in her mismatched bra and boy shorts the other night have nothing on this.

There's a faint sheen of sweat decorating her glorious skin, and I'm overcome with the need to trail my tongue from one delicious droplet to the next.

"Alex?"

"Um, what?"

"I asked, what is this?" Tuesday says, sipping from the frozen concoction I ordered for her.

"Oh." My voice cracks. "It's a Bahama Mamma."

"It's good," she coos, running her tongue over her bottom lip as she pulls the paper straw away from her mouth. Jesus. I'm going to need to dive into the pool before she sees how hard I am. *What the hell is wrong with me?*

Who am I kidding? I've been feeling a spark between us for a long time. It's part of the reason I started dating Ainsley. I needed something to distract me from the one girl I can't have.

I shouldn't have brought Ainsley here. I knew Tuesday had feelings for me. And the hurt I saw in her eyes when I so callously blurted "Fuck no" the morning she questioned if we'd had sex has haunted me. But Ricky mentioned the cruise in front of Ainsley. And to be honest, I'm quickly getting to the point I don't trust myself around this beauty queen anymore. She's going to have to stay firmly locked in my dreams where she belongs.

Shit. What?

"What did you get?" Her voice seems louder all of a sudden, and I look up to find she's bent over her chair, attempting to straighten her towel, her glorious, perky, full tits practically in my face. Beads of sweat collect on the nape of my neck, and I know it has nothing to do with the Miami heat.

I almost tell her I have blue balls, *that's what I got*, when Ainsley takes this opportunity to plop herself down on the end of my lounge chair and thrusts a bottle of sunscreen into my face.

It's official. I'm in hell.

Chapter 10

Alex

"Wow. I've never slept better than on this ship," Tuesday shares stretching her arms overhead dramatically as we all sit enjoying a late breakfast. Our table accommodating eight sits beside a large window overlooking the ocean. The buffet is enormous, offering anything one could imagine to start their day. Eggs, sausages, various croissants, pastries, and fruit sit atop our bright-colored plates.

"I need a lot more coffee," Ricky splutters. He and I stayed up late into the evening, checking out the nightlife onboard the ship. The girls all retired early after a full day of sun and alcohol.

"You feeling your age, old man?" I chuckle.

"Where's Ainsley?" Julia asks.

"She was still sleeping when I left." I take another sip of my coffee and have to admit I'm relieved for the non-Ainsley portions of this cruise. This relationship has more than outlived its course. I don't know what I was thinking, bringing her along. At this point, I'm clearly using her to play interference. How ridiculous is that? *Man up, Alex. Sunny T is never gonna happen. You don't need to drag another girl into this.*

The thought has barely left my mind before I notice the faces opposite me all staring over my shoulder, mouths ajar. My eyes follow where they have their gaze trained and observe none other than Ainsley walking down the corridor toward us, dressed for the runway. She's wearing some sheer floral coverlet over a bejeweled turquoise one-piece, four-inch heels, a rattan purse, and oversized sunglasses. Her platinum blonde hair is tied tightly to her head in an uncomfortable bun. I instinctively look about the café for her paparazzi. *Is this chick for real?*

She slinks into the seat beside me, and I almost slide down so no one realizes we're together. The rest of us are wearing T-shirts and cut-off shorts. "Ains, what's with the getup? It's kinda early for stilettos," I whisper.

"I'm on vacation. I want to enjoy myself," she quips with more than a little attitude. "I have a full day planned. I'm hitting the spa and getting the full package before I spend the afternoon sunbathing."

So, this outfit is to impress the women at the spa? I mean, you're just taking all of that off in there, right? I can't wrap my head around her logic. But it seems neither can anyone else at this table by their expressions.

"Maybe I want to look good for my man?" She croons as she cups my cheeks, and I try not to choke on a cough.

Good grief. This is karma for bringing her here. I'm sure of it.

"Mom and I are going to tour the ship and catch up on some reading on the observation deck before dinner," Dad says.

"Oh, that's right. You two have that romantic dinner in the exclusive restaurant tonight," Tuesday adds. "I'm probably going to spend most of the day sunbathing. But I'm going to take a nap before dinner this time so I can have fun tonight without falling asleep." She giggles.

I glare at her. Sunbathing nearly did me in yesterday. Maybe I should go to the gym.

———

JULIA, RICKY, TUESDAY, AND I RELAX WITH AFTER-DINNER drinks as the sun sets on another fun-filled day. Ainsley barely made it to the appetizer before the ship started rocking to and fro with a little more turbulence than we'd noticed previously and turned green, excusing herself. Ricky jumped into action, stating his parents had brought some sea sickness medication that would settle her stomach and escorted her back to her room to retrieve it.

"She'll be out for the count now," Ricky joked upon his return. "That stuff will keep you from spewing, but it could knock out an elephant."

I shake my head, trying not to voice what I'm thinking. She and her outfits need a good rest.

As I take the last sip of my coffee, Ricky and Julia spring to their feet, deciding to call it an early evening. I have no doubt what's on the agenda there.

"See you in the morning," Tuesday says as she gives them a small wave.

"So, what've you got planned tonight?" I nudge her with my elbow.

"Ah, Tuesday. I haven't seen you all day!" An overly cheerful voice rains down upon us, and my hackles rise as I look up to see the familiar face of her dark-haired dance partner from yesterday. I notice his nametag. Fitting. Rico Suave is actually Ricardo. "Are you coming dancing later?"

"No," I bark. Her eyes snap to mine, and I don't even bother backing down. "We've got plans."

"We do?" she whispers, seeming as shocked by my outburst as I am.

"You said you wanted to take in the nightlife on the ship. So that's what we're doing."

"Yes. You should," Ricardo adds. "Maybe I'll see you out and about later. Enjoy your evening."

Tuesday continues to give me a stunned expression.

"Come on, Sunny. It's just you and me. Let's live a little."

What the hell am I doing? Off-limits, remember.

Before I can think better of this and tell her I should probably call it a night and take a cold shower, a bright smile inhabits her face, and any hope of doing the rational thing is completely lost.

"What should we do? It's still kinda early for the clubs," she asks.

"Hmm. Why don't we start at the top of the ship and work our way down?"

"Oh, I love that idea." She claps in excitement. We stand from our seats, and my skin sizzles under her touch as she grabs my forearm. As we near the elevator, she lets go and reaches for the button, and I instantly mourn the loss of her.

This isn't good. The night has barely started, and you're already obsessed with having her hands on you.

The elevator doors open, and we squeeze in with the guests already onboard. "Oh, look. They have a volleyball court on the top floor." Tuesday points to the picture of the top floor of the ship. "Not that I'd ever be able to beat the local league volleyball champion." She giggles.

"God. I haven't played in ages." Man, I've missed it. I felt alive when I was attacking the ball.

The doors open, and we follow the signs to the sports area mid-ship. "I used to love watching you play," she admits, a slight blush staining her tanned cheeks. Her hair continually whips about her sweet face despite her attempts to tuck it behind her ear. "You were a god on the court."

Her statement has me standing a little taller. I'm startled by the compliment. Regardless of any infatuation she may have had back then, she never put a voice to it. I thought she was only there to watch Ricky play. Has she had more to drink tonight than I thought?

Reaching for a ball, I start to ask if she wants to toss it back and forth for a bit until I recall we just came from dinner. My eyes trail down her body. Unlike Ainsley, who uses any opportunity to dress to impress, Tuesday is wearing what I think they call a maxi dress and a pair of canvas wedges. Her hair is in loose waves, the strands haphazardly dancing in the wind around her.

"Come on. Lob that sucker, for old times' sake," she says as she kicks off her shoes and runs to the opposite side of the court. The grin that overtakes me is instantaneous. I extend my arm to prepare for my serve when she adds, "Be gentle."

Fuck. I'm going to be hearing that in my sleep now.

⸺

It's ten o'clock, and we've finally made our way down to the floor that houses multiple nightclubs. My face hurts from how much I've laughed and smiled tonight. From watching Tuesday chase after each serve, the way her cute nose scrunched up when she'd try my scotch, and the gusto with which she won the trivia game earlier. I can't remember the last time I had this much fun. The only uncomfortable moment I've experienced was when we were eating soft serve ice cream, and a small amount dribbled down her chin. It took all I had not to lick it off of her.

"Oh, this one, Alex." Tuesday pulls at my arm. This floor has several spots to kick back and enjoy a drink. One is sports-themed, there's a jazz club, an Irish pub, and this appears to be one of the dance clubs. The room is teaming with people, but she locates an empty booth in the back corner and points, looking in my direction in a silent plea. She's aware nightclubs aren't my thing.

We've barely taken our seats before a server is at our side. "What can I get you?" he practically yells over the rumbling hip-hop song.

"Whatcha want, Sunny T?"

"I dunno. I want to try something new. How about a mudslide?"

"Nice choice," the waiter answers with a wink. *Watch it, bucko.*

"I'll just have a water."

The server walks away, and Tuesday blurts, "What?" She looks offended.

"I'm driving, babe."

She covers her mouth with her hand and giggles, and the sound travels right to my dick. I can't help but grin as she looks about the club, her face aglow with the flashing lights overhead. But it could honestly be her. There's a luminosity about this beautiful, sweet girl.

The server returns quickly with our drinks, and I sit back, enjoying the sight of Tuesday tasting her next concoction. Her face becomes animated as the cool cocktail hits her lips. Her tongue darts out, running along her lower lip, and I have to reach down to readjust my pants.

I'd give anything to taste those plump lips. Dip my tongue into her mouth and lose myself in her.

"Want some?" she asks, her voice a little raspy.

"Yes," I answer before I realize what I'm saying. I reach for her drink, having no interest in chocolate in a glass but needing to follow this through so she doesn't question what I really want to taste. Bringing it to my lips, I take a small sip before sliding it back to her. "Delicious."

Tuesday suddenly sits up taller in her chair and bounces as the song changes to an eighties dance number. "Oh, Alex, please? Don't make me dance by myself," she pleads. That's the problem. She won't be. This stunner won't be out there a hot minute before someone slides in, hoping to keep her company.

"Okay, okay."

"Oh, yay!" She squeals. She reaches for my hand, dragging me into the center of the heap of warm bodies dancing to the popular song before it changes to an upbeat Andy Grammer song. Tuesday is in her element. A wide smile has permanently taken up residence on my face as I watch her. She dances with a look of glee I've never seen on her before. And that's saying something, given she's the most joy-filled girl I know. Her mesmerizing green eyes dance with delight as the song changes, and she begins gyrating her curvy body to "THAT'S WHAT I WANT" by Lil Naz X. I instinctively place my hands on her tantalizing hips as we get caught up in the chorus and move to the upbeat song.

With each passing tune, I fall a little more under her spell. I'd normally be running for the table, having done my duty dancing with her for a couple of numbers as requested. But the thought of having to pull away from her keeps my feet rooted to this dance floor.

"Alex," Tuesday says in a swoony tone as she grabs my shirt and pulls me into her.

"Yeah, baby?"

"This has been the best night of my life." The radiant spark emanating from her has short-circuited my mind. Any resolve I had left is gone.

I cup her angelic face and crush my lips over hers. The instant heat that spreads from her sweet mouth has me coming undone. I tease her lips with the tip of my tongue, begging for entrance. Once inside, it's impossible to know whether the moans I hear are coming from her or me. I can feel the current as the glide of her playful tongue connects with mine all the way down my spine. I pull her closer, enjoying the feel of her body engulfed by mine, and pray I can neutralize the electricity building between us.

Yet any hope of fighting this is pointless. No kiss has ever felt like this. All that came before was merely a means to an end. Foreplay to get what I really wanted. But this kiss with Tuesday. It's intoxicating. She tastes of chocolate, sunshine, and surrender.

I could spend eternity kissing this sweet girl.

This sweet, forbidden girl.

Chapter 11

Tuesday

The best night of my life is followed by the longest day I can remember. Alex walked me to my stateroom after the kiss of all kisses. I didn't want to ruin how magical the whole evening had been with an uncomfortable conversation about what it meant. But apparently, it meant nothing, as what little I saw of him today was aloof and uncomfortable.

Ainsley was by his side during much of the day, so I made excuses to find things to do elsewhere. It was too painful to see them together and try to pretend last night didn't happen.

Sure, I am somewhat to blame. I knew he wasn't available and let my mind and body go there anyway. The way we danced was inappropriate, but after all the years of pining for him, I couldn't stop myself. I'd honestly never been happier. It was silly to think any of it was real.

But I can't blame his behavior on too much alcohol. I was the one who'd been drinking all evening. He was only drinking water. And he's always been so quick to keep his distance. The only time there was any question was the morning I woke up in his arms. Yet he made it painfully clear what happened was platonic.

But that kiss. There's no faking something like that. Is there?

Does Alex Bell kiss everyone that way?

———

"CHEERS TO A GREAT WEEKEND," DAD SAYS AS WE ALL clink our champagne glasses.

It *had* been a great weekend. But what did I think was going to happen? Alex is here with his girlfriend.

"It's a shame Alex and Ainsley aren't here," Mom says.

"I think they wanted to have a romantic dinner together before the cruise was over," Dad tosses out over his Beef Wellington.

I put my utensils down, feeling heartsick. I've lost my appetite at the thought of them together.

"She probably had an outfit hanging in her closet that hadn't gotten any attention," Ricky mutters before Julia elbows him in the ribs.

"Be nice," she says under her breath.

"I don't really get what he sees in that one," my mother whispers, leaning into me.

I can't make eye contact with anyone, or I worry I'll tear up. What was I thinking, allowing my mind to dream of something happening with him? He's a player. That's just what he does, right? Years of longing have clouded my brain. That and that hypnotizing kiss.

I take a few more nibbles of my entrée, pushing my

food about my plate wanting to escape to my room. Leaning in toward my mother, I say, "I'm not feeling well. I think all of the sun and rich food has caught up with me. I think I'll get a jump start on packing up for tomorrow and get a good night's sleep."

"Oh, honey. Do you want me to come with you?"

"No. Enjoy your dinner. I'm okay. It's been a great trip. Thank you for everything." I stand from my chair and head to my stateroom after a chorus of goodnights. I'm giving myself this one night to cry it out. One night. Once I get off this ship, I'll leave my memories of last night and Alex Bell behind.

Chapter 12

Alex

"You're breaking up with me?"

I knew this would go down this way. All day I tried to devise the best way to end this. It would've been much simpler to do on land. Yet there was no way I could explain why I didn't want to have sex with her. It was our last night on the ship, and I'd barely touched her beyond holding her hand or a kiss on the cheek the whole trip. But I needed to rip the band-aid off once and for all.

Avoiding deep and meaningful conversations with Ainsley until we made it back to our stateroom for the evening wasn't tricky. I decided to take her to dinner, hoping it would soften the blow. She had an excuse to wear another outlandish outfit and spend the entire evening focusing on about her favorite subject. *Her*.

"Ainsley, this just isn't working anymore. This never supposed to be serious. You were okay with casual when we first started going out. But now we spend every waking breath together. I'm just not ready for all of this."

"We can go back to casual. I thought you liked spending time with me, that's all."

"Ainsley, you're a nice girl. But you like the party scene and dressing up to go out with your friends. I'm the total opposite. I'm stonewashed jeans, and you're Chanel."

"Chanel is so last decade," she huffs.

"See. You're making my point. I don't know one designer from the other."

"Well, it's only because I study fashion in college. Of course, you wouldn't know them. I could teach you."

"I don't want to know them. That's the point. You deserve to be with someone who enjoys giving you opportunities to get dressed up. Show you off. This cruise was a one-off. I would've never done this for the two of us. It was merely because the Palmers invited us to celebrate Tuesday's birthday." I wince as I complete the sentence. I can't take any chances she'll put two and two together and discover my feelings for the youngest Palmer are why we're breaking up.

Ainsley was a fun time. Until she wasn't. I hate that it ever came to this. I should never have taken it beyond friends with benefits. I admit her looks and the need to focus on someone other than my best friend's off-limits little sister allowed this to morph into more than I wanted. But this girl is not only shallow but spiteful. She has no problem causing drama if it gets her more attention. And I can't allow Tuesday to fall victim to her.

Picking up the pillow from my side of the bed, I head over to the narrow couch and plop down.

"What are you doing?"

"I don't expect you to want to sleep in the same bed after I called it quits with you."

Ainsley slinks in my direction, dropping her hands on my chest. "Awe, come on. One more night, for old times' sake?"

"No," I blurt.

"Are you for real?"

"Ainsley. There's no sense pretending. I don't want to send any mixed signals. We're done."

"Well, I hope you aren't sniffing around Tuesday. That frigid bitch could never give you what I can."

I had to bite the inside of my cheek to keep from lashing out at her. But I can't give my feelings for Tuesday away in anger. "Don't you dare talk about my friend that way, Ainsley."

She spins on her tall, pointy heel and stomps toward the door. "On that note, I'll end my vacation having a little fun. Now that I'm no longer tied down."

She hurls a sweatshirt hanging from a hook by the door at me before flinging the door wide and storming out.

In her absence, I seize the opportunity and pack up my things. I plan to disembark the minute the ship docks and we're allowed off. Hopefully, I can hop on an earlier flight on standby if a seat opens. I'll even cough up my savings to upgrade Ainsley's ticket so she can fly business class on a later flight to avoid the Palmers altogether. I really should've waited until we were home for this break-up. Holy shit, the lengths I'll go to in order to avoid having to sleep with her again.

Yet Ainsley is just one piece of this messy puzzle. I'll never believe that kiss was a mistake. But Ricky will never approve of me dating his sister. And do I want to risk giving up the Palmers if a relationship with Tuesday didn't work out? They mean a lot to me. I'm the youngest of four kids and the only boy. I'm constantly treated like a child when I'm with my family. I love them, but I feel at home with the Palmers. Heck, I've spent the last few Christmas dinners with them.

Moving forward with Tuesday is going to take a lot of careful consideration. I'm not the relationship type. My focus has been on my fire career and my friends. I've only ever dated casually until one of them says they want more. But I know there'd be nothing cavalier about dating Tuesday. I can safely say I'd turn into a possessive beast if I ever saw another man's hands on her.

Yet, staying away is getting more and more difficult.

After that kiss, she's all I can think about. How do I move on from this?

Chapter 13

Tuesday

Slosh. Slosh. Slosh. My boots make an unpleasant, wet, slurping sound as I trudge through the cold slush to my car. While the blanket of fresh snow on the trees and grass is pretty, it's just a dismal mess everywhere else. This overcast, almost gray day matches my mood. I'm a far cry from Miami now.

I haven't heard from or seen Alex since we returned from our trip. Not only did he not join us for dinner the last evening, but he and Ainsley disembarked without even saying goodbye to anyone. My heart hurt worse than it had waking up with him the morning after that squad party. The last time he quickly dismissed any consideration of something physical between us.

I'd dreamt of a night like that with Alex for years, yet I won't allow myself to replay that kiss. While I'll never regret it, his rejection has stung more than a little. It never ended up like this afterward in my dreams. It's as if the magic of that one incredible night with him onboard that ship is utterly tainted by the days that followed.

Starting my car, I rub my hands up and down my arms. The chill is sinking into my bones. I let the heater warm up before backing out. I'm leaving an hour early to ensure I make it to my volunteer job in the inclement weather. It'll be a busy night for the rescue squad with this early mix of precipitation. While there wasn't a lot of accumulation, and it doesn't seem overly icy, this can be the most deceiving type of winter weather. People underestimate the risk when the temperature drops and the wet roadways turn to black ice.

I turn up the radio to hear Sia over the repetitive swish of the snow-laden wiper blades. The snowfall has lightened, but each heavy, wet flake looks the size of a golf ball as it smacks against the windshield. I find myself leaning forward as if this will help me see more clearly through the cold, soppy mess.

Whoosh. My car swerves a bit as the eighteen-wheeler flies by me on the highway, adding a new layer of dirty, mushy spray over my car. Just when I feel as if I've righted myself, the front end of my car veers into the other lane and spins as I overcorrect the steering wheel. I can't help but let out a scream as my car flies off the highway onto the shoulder and collides with a metal guardrail.

My heart is hammering in my chest. *Get a grip, Tuesday. You're okay.* I reach to turn off the ignition when I realize the car is no longer running. *Great.* Stepping out of the car, I walk around the front end and see the damage to the passenger side isn't terrible. But if I can't get the car to start back up, there may be something worse going on underneath the hood. What's more, I'm going to need a tow.

Sloshing back to the driver's seat, I attempt to restart the car without success. Ugh. I pull out my phone, and as if on auto-pilot, I begin to call Alex. He's always been my go-to for anything car related. Not only does Alex have a tow truck business he runs on his days off from the fire department, but he's also just a wiz with cars. My brother, not so much.

Yet the reality of our current situation becomes clear, and I refuse to ask him for help after he ghosted me following that kiss. Okay, so maybe ghosted isn't the right word. I knew he was in a relationship. I was in the wrong too. But there's still no way I'm calling him.

Hitting Grace's number on my contact list, I tap my foot on the floorboard, praying she's home.

"Hey, girl. Whatcha doing? Hot chocolate and romcoms?"

"I wish." I shiver. "Does your brother still have that big SUV with all-wheel drive? I just slid off of the highway on Route One near Atlee Road on the way to my volunteer job, and now the car won't start back up."

"Yeah. But why don't you call Alex?"

"Grace, I told you what happened. I'm not calling him." I'd shared everything with Grace the night after my return. I tried to downplay how much it hurt and focused on my amazing night with him. I refused to shed any more tears over this ridiculous crush.

"Tues, he's your friend. He'd want to—"

"Grace, I don't have much battery left on my cell. I'm going to have to call someone else if your brother isn't there."

"Oh, okay. I'll get him. Put your phone on low battery and hang in there. Someone will get to you soon. Promise."

"Thanks." I hang up the call and reach into my backseat for the duffel bag I use for the rescue squad. It has some medical supplies if I should ever respond to a call from home, a few granola bars, a bottle of water that appears frozen solid, and a sweatshirt. I pull the thick gray sweatshirt over my head and pray they get here quickly.

"Hello?"

"Hi, Max. This is Tuesday. I was on my way there when I hydroplaned and hit a guardrail. I'm okay, but I'm waiting on a ride. I just wanted to let you know I'm probably going to be late."

"Oh, it's okay. I'm glad you're all right. We could definitely use the help, though, if you can still make it. We've had one call after another today, and most are car accident or fall related."

"I understand. I'll get there as soon as I can. I have to go. My phone battery is almost dead."

"Okay. Be careful. See you when you get here."

Hanging up the call, I drop the phone into my bag and again attempt to warm up my body by rubbing my hands up and down my arms and legs. I'm so distracted by my efforts to fight the chill that I scream like the scene of a horror movie when someone knocks on my window. My hands fly to my heart, and panic sets in as I can't see through my window now.

"It's me, Sunny. Open the door."

What? Slowly, I push the car door open to find Alex leaning against the car. He's wearing thick overalls, heavy Timberland boots, and a red and black flannel shirt. A beanie covers his thick dark hair, so all I see is his beautiful dark eyes and dreamy smile. "Hi." My voice comes out broken after that scream. I'm going to kill Grace.

"You okay?"

"Yeah. Just cold. I have squad duty tonight. They really need all hands on deck with this weather." My voice is shaky. I'm sure this is due to the cold, not his nearness. I'm too mad at him to let him affect me anymore.

Before I can give this any further consideration, he steps forward, reaching into the car, and scoops me into his arms in one swift motion.

"Alex—"

"Hush." He carries me to his truck, parked on the shoulder directly in front of mine. Dropping me onto my feet, he reaches for the door handle and pats my backside, encouraging me to climb in. Any other time this would do all sorts of things to my brain, but I'm so overwhelmed with his being here I can't think clearly.

Once I'm seated, he steps up and buckles me in. The smell of diesel fuel is replaced by an earthy, masculine scent that has me swooning as it envelopes me. It's so him. As the metallic click of the seatbelt snaps into place, my eyes flick up to meet his. He tucks a damp tendril of hair behind my ear with his snow-covered glove. The action makes me jump, but I'm again unsure if it's the connection with the cold mitt or him that's causing me to be so jittery.

It's the cold, Tuesday. He's not getting to you again.

"Sit tight. I'll be right back." He descends to the ground, closing the door behind him, and I watch through the rear window as he starts gathering what he needs to secure my car to the truck. He manages to lift my car behind the tow truck and returns to the driver's seat in no time.

"I can't believe you did that so fast. And by yourself."

"I've had a lot of practice." He winks. The action sends my heart into overdrive. What is happening here? Are we just going to ignore the elephant in the truck?

I train my gaze on the road in front of us, trying not to let my mind wander to places that are best left alone.

Besides, my tears might freeze solid once I leave the warmth of his vehicle.

Alex carefully steers us off of the shoulder and onto the highway when his voice breaks the silence. "Sunny. We need to talk."

Chapter 14

Alex

God. I'm not prepared for this. I went with my friend Mick to visit a friend in North Carolina for a few days, hoping the mountain air would clear my head. While it's gorgeous there, all I could think about was how much Sunny would like it. I tried to force myself to consider the pros and cons of starting a relationship with my best friend's little sister. But neither side seemed to win out. I feel stuck.

Returning home hadn't given me any clarity either. And as much as I knew I needed to talk to Tuesday about what happened on the ship, I wanted to wait until I'd thought this through carefully and could come up with the right words to say to her.

Yet when Grace called telling me Tuesday was in trouble, I was out the door before giving it another thought. That right there should be my answer. She's worth whatever risks come with dating her. The big question is, can I have a relationship with her, or anyone, for that matter, without hurting them in the end?

"What do we need to talk about?"

Is she kidding? There's no way I'm alone in this. "That kiss."

"Oh, it was nothing. We just got caught up in the night. That's all. I'll never speak of it. You don't have to worry about Ainsley finding out."

My hand immediately covers hers. I'm surprised I still feel a zing of electricity, given we're both wearing sopping wet gloves.

"Sunny, I'm sorry."

Tuesday

Here we go. This is where he lets me down gently. Well, too many days have passed for gentle.

"I shouldn't have done that with Ainsley still in the picture. I never want you to be in the middle. I'm sorry I couldn't control myself."

And there it is. My head drops down to our hands as my stomach lurches.

"Please don't take what I'm saying the wrong way. It wasn't a mistake. I've wanted to kiss you for a long, looooong time. It's just complicated. And I don't cheat. You and your brother may think I'm some sort of player, but I'm not like that."

My face snaps to his, and I have to admit, I believe I missed most of what he just said.

"Sunny?"

"You've wanted to kiss me?"

"Yes." I feel another gentle squeeze from his hand. "But this isn't smart. Your family means everything to me. And Ricky is like the brother I always wished I'd had.

Beyond him thinking I'm not good enough for you, I don't want to lose any of you if it doesn't work out for us. And I have no experience with relationships, so the odds are good *against* us not making it."

What? He's actually thought about this? "I guess none of this matters anyway. If you're with Ains—"

"I broke up with her on the ship. That's why we left early. I didn't want her picking up on any interactions between you and me and connecting it to the break up. She's a catty, spiteful girl who'll only tear you down to gain attention masked as sympathy. You didn't do anything. But I don't want you caught in the crosshairs."

Reflecting on his statement, I have to admit he's right. She's no stranger to *Real Housewives* worthy drama at the rescue squad. There have been more than a few girls who've quit over her behavior. I don't know why people tolerate her. But I guess there are mean girls everywhere. I've just been oblivious because I don't hang with that crowd. I guess that's one thing I can thank my overprotective family for.

We pull into the rescue squad parking lot, and I try to refocus on the task at hand. I have a responsibility to do my job, and I'm already late. "Thank you. Will you let me know where my car ends up so I can contact them about the repairs?"

"Sunny, wait."

"I have to go. Thank you for telling me everything." While I'm relieved I wasn't rejected after all, it does little to change the fact he doesn't want to pursue anything with me because of my family. I can't allow myself to swoon over any feelings he may or may not have for me if they aren't strong enough to force his hand.

"I'll be back after I drop your car off."

"You don't have to do that."

"Yes, I do. Your brother would kill me if I didn't look out for you."

I can't help but wince.

"Sunny." He grabs my hand again. "I'm sorry. I've hidden behind your brother for so long it's almost a habit to say that. I *want* to help you. I'll be back in a little while."

"But why? I'm on duty until six in the morning."

"I'm not leaving you here without a way home. And if a call for a tow comes in, I can respond from here as well as anywhere else. Heck, I'll be an ambulance chaser. If you respond on a call where someone needs me, give them my card." He winks again.

Stop that. You aren't helping my situation with that panty-melting wink. "Be careful. I'll see you later."

Tuesday

"Good grief. I hope it slows down soon," Hudson bellows. "This is exhausting. I'm glad enough of us were available tonight to staff three ambulances so we can take turns."

"Maybe now that it's gotten late, people will use some common sense and stay home," Max adds.

"Common sense? What's that?" A familiar voice interjects.

"Alex," Max and Hudson greet simultaneously, holding out their hands to shake.

"Come to join us?" Allison asks, twisting her hair around her forefinger playfully.

"Well, not to respond on squad calls. Tuesday needed

some help with an assignment due for class, and I need to give her a lift home since her car is now in the shop."

A dejected pout crosses Allison's face at his fictitious reply. Heck. I get it. I'm the poster child for dejected right now.

"You ready?" Alex directs toward me, and I almost forget the ruse he's just created for being here. "Grab your backpack. Let's get to work before another call steals you away."

"Okay." I follow him toward the bunk rooms. It's getting late, and I'm irritated I didn't think ahead to bring more than two granola bars with me. We normally stop to grab dinner but haven't had a chance with all of the commotion.

Walking inside, I drop my backpack onto the twin bed along the wall as he plops down on the one opposite. Alex reaches into his heavy, oversized coat, retrieves a white paper bag, and tosses it to me.

"What's this?"

"I figured you hadn't had a chance to eat. It's a turkey and cheese sub from Fancy Nosh."

"Oh, I love that deli. I could kiss you right now." My hand instantly flies to my mouth. I can't believe I just said that.

"Ugh. You have no idea how much I want that. I've replayed that kiss over and over."

He has? Suddenly, food is the last thing on my mind. "Do you find me attractive?"

"Jesus, Sunny. Of course I do. But your brother would kill me if I ever put my hands on you."

Out of the blue, I'm feeling more brave than I ever have before. Any thoughts of food are tossed to the side. I want to be like the girls I've seen make their move on what they want here. *Or who they want.* Like the Ainsleys and Allisons of the world who take no prisoners.

Quickly I stand, kicking off my shoes, watching his curious eyes follow my every movement as I unzip my white squad coveralls and lower them down my body. I place them and my shoes at the foot of the bed to don at a moment's notice if the tones of an incoming call should blare out. We were the last ambulance to take a call, so we should get a bit of a reprieve. I take a breath, trying to steady my nerves. I can't believe I'm doing this.

Lying back on the bed, feeling the weight of his heavy stare upon me, I turn and look in his direction. "Who said anything about *you* putting your hands on me?" I slide my hands into my top and massage my breasts.

"What the?" An audible gulp floats from his bed to mine.

I push forward, arching my back, deciding it's all or nothing now. I slide my right hand seductively from my shirt down into my leggings.

"Jesus, Sunny. What are you doing?"

"I'm tired of waiting. I have needs too. If you won't touch me, I'll do it. Unless you'd rather I find someone—"

"No," he blurts. "Fuck. This is dangerous."

I make a show of fiddling with my panties so he's fully aware I'm skin-to-skin and not touching myself through my underwear. Closing my eyes so I don't die of mortification when he eventually stops me, I try to focus on my goal. I'm tired of the mixed signals. I want him to know I'm a red-blooded woman with needs. And that if he won't step up and fulfill them, he needs a clear visual when he considers someone else might.

An audible click breaks through the silence, and my eyes fly open to find Alex locking the door to the bunk room. My pulse hastens, and I bite down on my lower lip as he towers above me.

"Do you think about me when you're touching yourself?" he asks, his voice thick.

"Yes."

A clear groan lilts above me, causing my back to arch in response.

"Is your pussy wet for me?"

"Yes."

Another moan escapes his lips, and I notice his hands are balled into fists at his sides. "Slide your finger inside."

I can't help but pant at his request. I do as he asks and look up to find his normally chocolate orbs are almost black beneath his hooded lids.

"Are you a virgin, Sunny?"

"No."

It's difficult to read his expression. It's a mix of relief and confusion. But there's no time to ponder this as I'm immediately distracted by his large, muscular hand that's now rubbing at the prominent bulge in his pants.

My eyes roll back in my head, and I let out a whimper at the thought of him pulling out his cock and stroking it for me. I can't believe I'm doing this, but his reaction is everything I wanted and more. Well, short of ripping his clothes off and taking me here on this bed in a squad building full of people.

"I want to taste you."

This elicits an uncontrollable gasp. No one has ever made such a statement, much less actually done it.

"Let me see your fingers, Sunny."

What? I remove my hand from my panties and lift it peculiarly. Before I can consider whether to return to what I was doing, Alex leans forward, licking the pads of my fingers, and I struggle for breath.

"Fuck, you're sweet. You're killing me, Tues. Do you have any idea how badly I want you?"

"No," I answer honestly.

"Drop your fingers back down and finish the job, baby. I want to watch you come."

Oh. My. God.

Closing my eyes so I don't completely flake out, I slide my hand back into my panties and swirl the pads of my fingertips over my swollen clit. I'm literally throbbing right now.

The sound of metal teeth clicking beside me causes my lids to pop wide, and I turn to see Alex reaching into his black boxers. Even with his pants still on, I can tell he's big. My fingers dance feverishly over my wet folds as he strokes his concealed length beside me, my pace picking up each time the almost purple, wide crown of his dick peeks out of the top of his boxers.

"Alex," I whimper, trying to keep my voice low.

"Fuck, Sunny. I want to feast on you right now. Kiss those ruby red lips, suck from what I bet are the prettiest tits I've ever seen, and devour that sweet pussy until you're coming all over my face."

"Oh, god."

"Has anyone ever eaten you before?"

"No."

A delicious smirk lifts one corner of his mouth as he tugs harder on his cock.

"Alex, I'm…"

Squatting down by the bed, he places his mouth next to my ear. "Get it, beautiful girl. Come for me."

My body starts to convulse; the sounds of ecstasy tumbling from my lips are, I'm sure, far too loud for this public place. As if he's read my mind, his delicious mouth is on mine, swallowing my sounds as my shaking starts to subside.

"I need your hand, baby."

His words break through the fog, and I slide my hand free as I did earlier. Alex's lips wrap around my fingers, and his groan vibrates against my trembling hand. All of a sudden, he pulls them free as profanity collides with my palm. The sight of him is like nothing I ever imagined. With his eyes closed, head thrown back, Alex stills, moaning incoherently as I only assume he empties into his hand.

What on earth have we just done?

Chapter 15

Tuesday

"The annual rescue squad and fire banquet are coming up soon. Do you think Alex will take you?" Grace asks from her perch on the counter beside me at Cygnature Blooms.

I shared what had transpired after she called Alex to rescue me. Well, the abbreviated version. She doesn't need to hear the dirty details. Heck, I barely believe that happened. "I don't think he's interested in a relationship with me."

"What? Why?" she whines, tearing off the end of her red cherry Twizzlers.

"He had several reasons. For one, he isn't ready to risk the wrath of my brother." She rolls her eyes as if this is some sort of a cop-out. I admit I felt the same way before. "He's honestly worried if something didn't work out with us, he'd lose all of us. My brother, me, and my parents. They practically consider him a member of the family."

Grace tilts her head as if she's giving this serious thought.

"Plus, he is worried that if we did act on this now, Ainsley would retaliate."

"Crap. I never thought of that. He's right. She's a witch." She chomps down on her licorice vine once more. "So, are you going stag to the banquet? You better still be going. We've had dresses picked out for ages." While Grace doesn't volunteer at the rescue squad, she is friends with many of the people there and always manages to secure an invite from either a squad member or a firefighter.

I've given this a fair amount of thought since the debauchery in the bunk room. I'd never want to hurt Alex. But it took pushing the envelope with him to get him to respond to me. I'm sure plenty of people are afraid to take a risk on someone because of all the things that could go wrong. Yet, I've crushed on him for years. Watching him with other girls. I'm done waiting. "No. I want to find a date." I say, chewing on my nail. "He needs to decide if I'm worth the risk once and for all."

"Hot damn!" she squeals. "Well, I have just the date for you. Don't you worry about a thing, Tuesday, my dear. I've got this handled."

Uh oh.

━━━

IT'S THE NIGHT OF THE SQUAD AND FIRE GALA. I'VE probably second-guessed my decision to go with a date about a hundred times. But I'm not getting any younger. I haven't heard much from Alex beyond a few generic texts to see how I'm doing. It's as if he's at war with himself. Well, I refuse to be a casualty. If he decides I'm not worth it, then at least I can say I went down swinging.

Bzzz. Bzzz.

"Hello."

"Hey, chicka. We're here. You ready?"

I peer out my window to the driveway below and see a black, shiny Ford Explorer belonging to Gunner, Grace's date.

"Yeah, I'll be right there." I still don't know anything about my date for the evening. Grace just said she found him through someone at college, and he's a very hot, funny guy. I have no plans to separate from Grace this evening, so I feel safe attending the event tonight with a blind date. Even if it's a tad unnerving knowing nothing about him except 'he's cute, and he's always up for a good time.'

"Bye, Mom. Grace and I are crashing at Ricky's tonight after the gala while he's away." My brother managed to receive two offers for medical school and is in Norfolk, trying to secure an apartment before school starts at Eastern in two months.

"Okay, dear. You girls have fun."

As I approach the car, I see Grace waving from the front passenger seat when the door behind her swings open, and a tall, dark-haired man with deep blue eyes steps out to greet me. Holy hell. Where'd she find this guy? He's muscular but lean, dressed in a dark gray suit with a crisp white button-up and silver tie completing the ensemble. I dare say, if I wasn't already smitten with the man of my dreams, this guy would certainly have my undivided attention.

"Hi. You must be Tuesday. I'm Gavin." He holds out his hand to me, and I actually feel a little flushed.

"Hi, Gavin. It's nice to meet you. Thank you for doing this."

He gives me a deliberate look that starts from my heels and slowly drags up my body to my face. It feels as if he's undressed me with his eyes on the way up. "The pleasure is all mine, beautiful." Gavin extends his arm toward the open door, and I slide in, finding a corsage sitting where I assume he was moments ago.

"Is this for me?"

"Yes. Will you allow me to put it on?"

Is this guy for real? The most I've ever hoped for from guys I've dated at the rescue squad in the past was that their clothes didn't reek of the girl's perfume they dated before me.

We proceed to the venue, a downtown Richmond hotel, and I choose to remain quiet for now, watching the evening's scenery pass by the window. I don't want to use up all of my small talk with Gavin before we get there.

Once we park and take the skywalk from the garage to the hotel, Grace and I quickly check our coats and head into the ballroom. It's set up as usual, with multiple large circular tables accommodating ten people placed throughout the large room. This year's theme is black and gold, with the fire and EMS logos attached to decorative centerpieces on each table. EMTs and firefighters are mingling about in formalwear, waiting for dinner to be served. I'm a little sad that Ricky had to miss this. He always looks forward to these events, probably because he can always count on winning some award for responding to the most calls or the most volunteer hours logged.

I look about the space and don't see Alex. I do see Ainsley, however. She's all decked out in sequins, hanging on Curt's arm. He's a relatively new member to the rescue squad but already quite popular. He's a shoo-in to get into medical school with his grades and charisma. I'm sure latching herself onto his star will benefit her in the long run. I could definitely see Ainsley parading around as a doctor's wife.

An overhead announcement is made that dinner will begin shortly, followed by an awards ceremony, then dancing. In my few years attending, this is the usual routine.

Leaning into Gavin, I say, "This is going to get real boring, real quick." I laugh.

"Yeah, most of these things are all the same."

"Do you mind my asking how old you are?"

"I'm twenty. How about you?" he asks.

"I just turned twenty-one." I would've guessed he was much older with the way he carries himself. "If I forget to say it later, thank you. It was really nice of you to come here with me. I really owe Grace one for this."

He returns my smile with a curious smirk. *What's that about, I wonder.*

We sit down to the usual banquet food of rubbery chicken floating in some sauce I can't identify, a vegetable medley, and a baked potato that could second as a doorstop. Luckily, the banter about the table keeps the dinner moving along, and the awards ceremony is short. As the plates are removed, and the DJ begins spinning dance numbers, I take another look around. Still no sign of Alex. Perhaps he decided to skip this year's gala with Ricky being away.

"Would you like to dance?" Gavin asks.

Wow. Guys never seem to initiate dancing. I have to drag them onto the floor. I might as well enjoy the rest of the evening. "Sure. Why not?"

Alex

I hadn't planned to attend this banquet. Ricky's away, and I can't bring the one girl I want to spend the evening with. But I've been able to think of nothing but her since that night in the bunk room. My sweet, innocent Sunny had shocked me. So bold and unashamed, calling my bluff. She knew how much I wanted her, and now I'm tortured by the very clear visual of what I can't have.

Tuesday always seemed to come alive at the yearly squad and firefighter banquets. As with most girls, I'm sure it was a great reason to get dressed up and dance. I hadn't confirmed she was going, yet with the ticking of the clock, morbid curiosity had me putting on my suit, hopping in my truck, and driving downtown.

Only to find her all dolled up and dancing with another man.

There was no missing where Tuesday was in this crowd. Wearing an evening gown that makes her look like a Hollywood starlet, she stands out from all the rest on the dance floor. It's a beautiful jade form-fitting, floor-length dress. The color matches her eyes. There aren't any flashy sequins or a lot of skin showing as Ainsley would wear. It's sophisticated and timeless, just like my girl. Her hair tumbles over her shoulders in waves, and my hands itch to run my fingers through it.

Who is this guy? I know all of the players from fire, rescue, and the police department, for that matter. Word travels quickly in this town, making it nearly impossible to hide the romantic conquests that occur. The married police officers who are hitting it with the dispatchers. The brothers in the fire department from different stations who are unknowingly being played by the same fireflies. And don't get me started on the soap opera drama of EMS. But this guy is new.

Keeping my distance, I sip on a scotch and watch. He's respectful of her personal space but still entirely too close. Is this the kind of shit I'm going to have to succumb to for the rest of my life? Watching the girl who got away dance with someone else because I pushed her into their arms?

All because I was too chicken shit to go after what I wanted?

The dance number ends and is replaced by a slow song. Great. A Bruno Mars tune. As if on cue, her date pulls her in, and she sways to the music, her hands resting on his chest. At one point, she tosses her head back and laughs, and he smiles down at her. *Fuck, does he have two dimples to my one?*

I take another sip of my scotch, my jaw feeling so tight my teeth could start popping out of my face at any moment. Observing them, I'm unsure what to make of this. Has she already moved on? I'd have it coming if she did. Sure, I have a lot to lose if things go south with her, but isn't that the risk you take when you find the right girl? I'm twenty-five fucking years old. I can't keep ping-ponging from one meaningless relationship to another because I'm afraid of what might happen. It'd just be so much easier if the first time I was interested in a relationship, it was with someone else. Not my best friend's little sister and the daughter of the coolest parents ever.

All of a sudden, I see Tuesday's date tuck her hair behind her ear, leaning forward to whisper something, and I snap. Tossing back the rest of my scotch, I place the glass on a table and charge in their direction.

"Excuse me. Tuesday, I need to talk to you for a moment."

She barely pulls her eyes away from her date to answer me. "What about? I'm kind of in the middle of something."

"It's private. And it can't wait."

When did this girl get so sassy? She just fucking rolled her eyes at me.

"I'm sorry, Gavin. I'll be back."

Once we're in the hallway, I reach back for her hand and can't help muttering, "No, you won't." I continue walking down a long corridor toward the restrooms when I hear her say from behind me.

"What's this about, Alex? I haven't heard from you in—"

Unable to hold back any longer, I grab her arm and pull her behind an ornamental tree, pushing her up against the wall. My lips crash onto hers, and my body hums in appreciation of the much-needed connection. My tongue darts through her lips, her taste equal parts sweet and sinful as I devour her. Tuesday Palmer feels like the very air I need to breathe.

"I can't fight this any longer, Sunny. I surrender. Your brother will probably kill me once he finds out, and your family will lose all respect for me. But you're all I think about. And the thought of another man's hands on you is going to push me over the edge."

"What are you saying?"

I lean in so close you can't slide dental floss between us. Her gorgeous body fits me perfectly, her unique floral scent entrancing me like a drug. I've never felt this way before. So out of control. Is this what it's like when you're falling in love?

It's now or never, you idiot.

"I want it all with you, Sunny. If I have this chance and it doesn't work out… if I lose Ricky and your family when it's all over. It'll all be worth it. I'm sorry it's taken me so long to see that. I was just scared."

"Are you sure, Alex?" She crosses her arms over her chest, pushing her incredible rack further up her strapless gown, taunting me. "The Katy Perry hot and cold routine is getting old."

"I know. I'm sorry. We need to keep things under wraps a little longer to ensure Ainsley doesn't come after you. Plus, your brother leaves for medical school in a few months. I'd like to have a chance to spend time together before we break the news to him."

She pulls back from me, and my heart is suddenly in my throat. Is it too late? *I'll fucking beg if I have to.*

"You sound like you've given this a lot of thought."

"Baby, I think about little else. I never want you to think you aren't worth the risk. It's just a big step for me, committing to a long-term relationship. It's not just the fear of losing all of you. I needed to be sure I wouldn't hurt you. I know I'm going to screw this up. Look at what I've done to you already." I hang my head in shame, praying she'll have mercy on me and give me a chance.

I barely get the words out, and my sweet girl is flinging herself at me. Her kiss nearly knocks the lighted ornamental tree beside us to the ground.

"Come home with me?" I moan against her plush mouth.

"Yes."

"Get your things. I'll have the car waiting at the front."

"Okay."

"And, Sunny…"

"Yes."

"You better keep a chair between you and that date of yours when you say goodbye. If I see one more man with his hands on you, there will be no keeping our relationship secret. Because my fucking mug shot will be plastered all over the evening news when I'm arrested for murder."

Chapter 16

Tuesday

I can't believe this is happening. When I set this plan in motion, I hoped but never truly believed he'd take the bait. But he seems so sincere. Looking down at our entwined hands, it feels surreal after all these years.

As if he's heard my thoughts, he lifts my hand to his mouth and places a chaste kiss on my knuckles. "You look incredible, Sunny."

"Thank you," my words come out tremulous. I don't know if I'm feeling overcome by the magnitude of these events, the fact I'm headed to his place, or worry that it'll just end the way the other times have gone. I'm not sure I'll survive him walking away again.

"Are you okay?"

I nod, deciding we've had enough talk for one night. I have to acknowledge this and try to have faith. Although my worry is, the truth will reveal itself in the morning.

We arrive at Alex's apartment, and he quickly jumps out of his truck and comes to my door to help me down. As he takes my hand, it dawns on me. "All of my things are at Ricky's place. I was going to go there with Grace after the gala."

"What do you need? If it's something important, I can drive over and get it."

Looking down at my dress, I pop my hip. "I don't have anything else to wear."

He pulls me into his strong, muscular arms. "That's fine by me."

As much as I've dreamed of this moment, I don't want to have to put this back on in the morning.

"I'm teasing, babe. You can wear one of my shirts. Just message Grace and ask her to leave your bag by the door and I'll swing by early and get it."

"Are you sure? Grace will know where I was all night." I say each word succinctly, so there's no doubt he understands what I'm saying.

With a stern expression, he grabs my hands and takes a step back. "I want to get something very clear. I'm not hiding a relationship with you because I'm embarrassed. I'll shout it off the rooftops once we've told your brother. I only want the chance to actually be in a relationship with you before we share it with other people. So long as Grace will give us the opportunity to enjoy being a couple before she out's us, I don't care if she knows."

A couple. I'm stunned. I don't realize how obvious it is that I'm speechless until I feel Alex close my mouth, lifting my chin with his index finger.

"I know I've let you down. I really care about you. This is new for me. I want to get this right."

Wrapping my arms around his waist, I rest my cheek against his chest. His heart sounds as if it's mimicking mine, galloping like a racehorse. I feel his hand stroking my hair before he lays a gentle kiss on the top of my head.

"And don't be worried about staying with me. I just want to hold you. We don't have to do anything more until you're ready."

An overwhelming sense of relief washes over me. Not that I don't want to have sex with this god of a man. But it is moving so quickly, and it isn't helping that nagging sensation, wondering if I'll roll over tomorrow and all of this will be over.

Alex leads me to his apartment and opens the door, welcoming me into the main living area. It's a typical apartment, much like Ricky's. A living room and kitchen in the center, flanked, I assume, by two bedrooms. It's not overly masculine but still has a bachelor pad vibe about it. He reaches for my coat, startling me. "Don't be nervous. It's just me."

"I'm sorry, Alex. The last few times we've been together have kinda done a number on me."

His head drops, and as much as I feel bad about hurting him, I want nothing but transparency between us from here on out.

"You have every right to feel that way. All I can give you is my word. I'm all in. I've never felt this way about any woman before." He steps forward, taking my hands in his. "Sunny, I wouldn't risk my relationship with your brother, or you if I wasn't sure we were the real thing. I needed time to make sure it wasn't simply physical. If you were anyone else, I would've asked you out after the night at the party when we woke up together. But I had to be sure this was real. You mean too much to me to string you along."

Dropping his hands, I take a few steps back. He starts to look a little pale until I reach behind my dress to find my zipper. It takes some finesse, as getting the thing zipped up on my own was difficult, but thankfully, I reach it and slowly lower it enough that I can drop the slinky silk to the floor and step out of it.

"Jesus, Sun," Alex says as he wipes his hand down his face. Stepping forward, he scoops me in his arms and carries me down the hallway. Kicking the door open, he takes a few more steps before depositing me on the edge of his bed. "Lie back for me. Please? I want to look at you."

I start to kick off my nude-colored heels when he stops me.

"Leave them on. Please?"

Oh. I lie back, resting my head on his pillow as he stands beside me. I've never seen a hunger like this on anyone's face before. And it's for me.

Alex slowly slides his suit jacket off and drapes it over a chair in the corner before loosening his tie. My body starts quivering as he slides his crisp white shirt out and begins undoing the buttons.

I drag my tongue along my lips and rub my thighs together, feeling overcome with need. I've only ever had sex once, and it was what you might expect for your first time. Painful and over before it began, there was a lot of fumbling, a painful initiation into womanhood, and what I suspect may have been the quickest orgasm in history. Well, for him, anyway.

After that lackluster sexual encounter, I decided to stick to the self-love variety. The very idea that Alex and I might… This simply doesn't feel real.

Alex removes his starched dress shirt before moving to his belt. If my heart was racing before, it's at supersonic levels now. His gray slacks slide down his muscular legs, and he stands beside me, looking like an Adonis. He has firm pecs, rippled abs, and a thin line of dark hair that snakes from his navel down into his boxer briefs, where an enormous bulge lies beneath. Am I ready for this?

He trails a finger from my lips, down my neck, between my breasts, and down my stomach before stopping at the hem of my panties.

"I love yellow on you, Sunny." He's toying with the little white ribbon attached to my pale yellow thong. "Can I take this off?" His fingers move to my matching strapless bra. The timid sound of his voice gives away his nerves. It comforts me that I'm not alone in my jitters.

Biting my lower lip, I nod.

Alex climbs over me, straddling my hips as he leans forward to lick my collarbone and reaches behind to unsnap my bra. As he straightens, I hear an audible groan as he looks at my breasts. I expect him to cup them, yet he surprises me as he scoots back and reaches for my panties. "Is this okay? I want to be—"

"Yes."

Unmoving, he blinks for a moment as if he's giving me a chance to retract my answer.

"I want you."

Chapter 17

Alex

I have to swallow hard, convincing myself this is actually happening. Sliding my thumbs into the sides of her tiny yellow panties, I try to steady my quivering hands as I slowly glide them down her legs. Depositing them at the end of the bed, I take her in.

"You're the most beautiful thing I've ever seen."

Her cheeks have a slight pink hue that seems to travel down her neck toward the top of her chest. It's then I allow myself to fully appreciate the most glorious set of tits on the planet. They're perfectly round with tight peach-colored nipples. I'm dying to squeeze and suck from them, but my eyes drift down her body to her beautiful, swollen pussy. She's not shaved bare but has a small landing strip of hair. It's just as I'd imagined she'd be. My cock is so hard I'm surprised it hasn't torn through my boxers.

Tuesday trembles under my perusal as starts to cover her breasts with her hands.

"No, please. I'm sorry. I was just caught up by your beautiful body." Crawling back over her, I lean down to nuzzle her beautiful tits before cupping one with my hand and sucking from the other. Her whimpers above me are going to do me in. I want to make love to her all night. Show her with my body what I've been so terrible about showing with my actions. But I've fantasized about her for so long that I know this will never last as long as I'd like.

Reaching down, I stroke her soft core. She's soaked. God, I'd love to taste her, but it'll have me coming in my pants. I'm so revved up. I slide a finger inside and groan at how tight she feels.

"Sunny? When's the last time you were with a man?"

"Never."

My head flies up. I thought she said she wasn't a virgin.

"I've only had sex once. And he was a boy."

"When?"

"Prom." Her hands fly to her face in apparent embarrassment.

Moving quickly, I lie beside her. "It's okay. I just don't want to hurt you." I lean down to kiss her sweet mouth, her eyes still buried under her hands. Skating my fingers down her silky torso, I run them through her soft curls before dipping my finger back inside her. "You're so wet, baby." I lean in to kiss her again. "If you really want this, it's going to be okay."

"I do. I'm just embarrassed. I'm sure you're used to... well..."

"Stop. I've never slept with anyone I had feelings for. This is a first for me. There's no comparison."

Her hands drop from her face, and she gives me the sweetest smile.

"I want to make you happy, Sunny." I slide a second finger inside her, gliding them in and out, and watch as her back arches when I hit her sweet spot. "Spread your legs a little for me." As she complies, I insert one more. Her hands dig into the sheets as she adjusts to the fullness. Using my thumb, I tease her swollen clit, hoping to loosen her up a little more before attempting to enter her.

As she releases a couple of mewls, I ask, "Does that feel good?"

Biting into her lower lip, she nods. I lean toward my nightstand and reach for a condom.

"You sure, Tues?"

"Yes, please," she moans.

I sit up, sliding off my boxers before opening the foiled package.

Her eyes land on my cock, and her expression immediately turns to one of alarm. "That's never going to fit."

"Baby, it will. I'm going to go slow. We'll stop if I'm hurting you." I spread her thighs wide, placing the tip of my cock at her entrance, and have to force myself to exhale. The feeling of tight warmth that shoots from the tip of my dick throughout my body is like nothing I've ever experienced. With slow, punishing stabs, I inch myself into her snug body, praying I don't come before I'm halfway in. "Rock your hips back and forth, T."

She complies, although I can tell she's struggling to accommodate me.

"That's it. Let me in, baby."

As her expression softens, I continue to push forward, an inch at a time, until I'm fully seated. She feels like heaven on earth. "You okay?"

"Yes."

"Does it hurt?"

"It only burns a little."

With this, I slowly slide in and out of her, my eyes rolling back in my head at the feel of her body wrapped around me. Her little moans cause my pace to increase until I feel her nails digging into my ass. Looking down at my beauty, Tuesday's face appears consumed with lust. I let go of her legs, leaning to rest my weight on my arms as I thrust into her.

"Oh, Alex."

"Is it okay?"

"It's better than okay."

I take this as my green light and begin driving into her more aggressively. The sound of our wet flesh slapping together is pushing this climax faster than I'd like. But she feels too good.

"Oh, the things I want to do to your sweet little body. I knew I'd never last tonight. I've dreamt of this for so long. But I cannot wait to have my face buried between your thighs, sliding my fingers in and out of you while I'm sucking from that swollen little clit."

"Alex," she cries.

"Find your vibrator, and run it over your little bundle of nerves while my tongue is buried in your sweet, wet pussy."

"Alex!" Her nails are buried so deep in my ass I'm sure she's drawn blood. I pound into her relentlessly as she throws her head back, moaning unintelligibly. The sight of her is sending me careening over the edge.

"That's it, baby. Come all over me." Two more strokes and there's no holding back. "Oh, fuck. Sunny." My heart is about to tear through my chest. Collapsing beside her, I struggle to catch my breath.

As my pulse begins to slow, I reach over and brush her damp hair from her face. Leaning on my elbow, I kiss her forehead, her nose, and her lips. "I'll never forget this night. Ever."

Tuesday blinks up at me wordlessly.

Stroking her cheek, I kiss her again. "You okay?"

"Yes."

She's so quiet, and it's a bit unnerving. I gather her in my arms and coax her to give in to sleep. Hopefully, tomorrow will be the start of a new life for both of us.

Chapter 18

Tuesday

I wasn't dreaming. This actually happened. Waking in Alex's arms felt similar to the last time. Yet there was no trepidation this time. He held me tight, his morning wood buried between my ass cheeks, kissing the nape of my neck as he stirred.

It was as if I could finally exhale. And thank god. Because how do you have sex like that and ever think you can walk away?

Last night was overwhelming. I had no idea anything could feel that way. Between my euphoria, utter exhaustion, and fear that I'd wake up today and it'd all be over, I couldn't risk any meaningful conversation.

I'm far too sore to give morning sex consideration. Alex seemed to anticipate this as he brought me some Ibuprofen and a tall glass of water before jumping in the shower and heading to Ricky's to gather my things.

Grace squealed so loud in the phone at the news we were giving this relationship thing a go I thought my eardrum might've ruptured. When I thanked her again for finding Gavin to stir the pot, she said, "Merry Christmas and Happy Birthday. No, like, for real." I guess one day, I'll have to learn more about how she found him.

Once Alex returned, he made us breakfast, and we spent the remainder of the day watching Netflix, cuddled up on his couch. I hated the idea of returning home, but he had to report for work at six in the morning, and I had classes and work at Cygnature Blooms tomorrow. Besides, I'm fully aware I needed to take it slow with him. Neither of us had ever been in a long-term relationship. We'll have to pace ourselves if we don't want this blaze to fizzle out too quickly.

"I hope you enjoy that beautiful poinsettia, Mr. Roberts."

"Oh, I will, Tuesday. My wife is going to love it."

As the kind regular to our shop exits the front door, he lingers to hold it wide for a well-bundled Grace, who's carrying two coffee cups. "Holy cow. It's so cold."

"Christmas is in the air." I laugh.

"I'm thinking I'd prefer to feel Christmas in the air on a sunny island in the Caribbean."

I can't help but recall the cruise and that incredible night with Alex. I'd definitely like to make cruising to all sorts of destinations happen. Especially the tropical ones. "Do you have any plans for the holidays?" Unlike our home, where every single year is the same, Grace's family seems to alternate where the celebrations will occur.

"I'm not jazzed about going this year, to be honest. It's

at my Aunt Kittie's house. She has this big dog that's obsessed with me whenever I visit. There could be a house full of people, but that dog insists on following me around everywhere with his nose in my crotch."

A chuckle escapes. "He must like what you've got going on downtown."

"It's embarrassing. I stopped wearing dresses because it'd look like I peed myself when it was his damn wet nose."

Looking at the coffee cups Grace has deposited on the counter, I ask, "Did you make a coffee run?"

"No. It's hot chocolate." She rubs her hands together in excitement. "They were selling it at Fancy Nosh."

"Oh, yum. Thank you. Were you getting lunch there?"

"I'm actually applying for a job—"

Grace's words are interrupted by shrill sirens coming close to our shop. "Are we on fire?" She laughs.

We both make our way to the front window and watch as Hanover's finest pull into the parking lot, stopping next to a lone red BMW. The boys jump down from the bright red engine and head to the driver's door. Within minutes, another set of sirens is audible, and an ambulance arrives on the scene.

"What do you think's going on?" Grace asks.

"Looks like maybe the driver is having some sort of medical event."

"Why would they send a fire truck for that?" I'm surprised as much time as Grace spends with my EMT and firefighter friends, she hasn't learned more about how they operate.

"Fire is always dispatched on any medical call because there are more fire stations than volunteer rescue squads in the area. Basically, they can get there quicker and get care started until the ambulance arrives. It's particularly helpful if someone is in cardiac arrest, has a stroke, or has a heart attack. Time is precious."

"Oh. I never thought about that."

It suddenly hits me that Alex is on duty today, and our shopping center is in his immediate area. This thought is confirmed as my handsome secret boyfriend walks around the back of the engine to return to the driver's seat once EMS is on scene.

Alex is wearing his full turnout gear, likely because it's so cold. As if he's got mental telepathy, he removes his helmet, runs his hand through his wavy dark locks, looks directly at our shop, and gives me a wink.

"Um, Tues?"

"Yeah?"

"Is it considered cheating if your boyfriend just gave me an orgasm?"

Smacking her on the arm, I can't help but laugh out loud.

Yeah, my boyfriend is one hot tamale.

Chapter 19

Tuesday

It's Christmas morning, the happiest I can remember ever feeling. My family surrounds me, things are going better than I'd anticipated with Alex, and Ricky is preparing to leave for medical school in a few days.

It has been tough keeping my relationship with Alex under wraps over the last six weeks, but we only have a few more weeks to go before he plans to drive to Norfolk and break the news to my brother. He hopes our love life won't be such a big deal once Ricky is preoccupied with more important things.

"Look who's here," my mom calls from the front door. I can't help my grin. We all know who it is. It is how she greets Alex every holiday. It's hard not running to him. I've missed him. I haven't seen him in the last few days because of holiday festivities, my volunteer job, and our work schedules. Thank goodness I'm off of school for a few more weeks.

"Have you had breakfast, Alex?" Dad asks.

"Yes, sir. I had it early with my family. All of my sisters' kids were up early waiting to tear into what Santa brought." He chuckles, carrying several wrapped packages with him.

"Oh, those were the days," Mom says in a sing-song voice.

"Don't you two be in any hurry to start your own," Dad scolds.

Ricky shakes his head, knowing that's definitely out of the question for him. At least poor Julia is only a few hours away. But I know she wouldn't want any surprise pregnancy to happen that could stand in the way of Ricky's medical career. And there's no way I'm ready. Heck, we can't even tell anyone we're dating yet. Any thoughts of marriage and children aren't even on my radar.

Alex walks over to pat Ricky on the shoulder and hands him his gift. I don't know why they bother to buy each other gifts. They each exchange a gift card to a local restaurant with the other every year.

Then he walks over to me. I can feel my pulse jumping to the point I wonder if everyone else can see it. "Hey, Sunny T. Merry Christmas." He gives me a devilish wink and leans in to kiss me on the cheek before handing me his wrapped gift.

"Let me guess. It's a book," Ricky says.

My mother smacks him on the back of the head. "Hush."

As I gingerly remove the pretty paper, I find a beautiful copy of Jane Austen's *Sense and Sensibility*. My heart soars as he knows this is one I've been hoping for. Turning the pages with gold foil edging, I find a pretty bookmark with a dark background covered in sunflowers.

"Thank you, Alex. I love it."

"You're welcome." His grin is infectious.

Ricky shakes his head at Alex's predictable gift. Every year, it's a different classic. But until this year, I didn't realize how much he'd paid attention to my conversations about my favorite authors. He'd let it slip one night when we'd been watching a movie adaptation of Jane Austen's *Persuasion*, that some years he'd have to pry it out of me when he couldn't pick up any clues during conversations with my mother.

Flipping the bookmark over, I bite my lip to prevent gasping. Tucked into the plastic sleeve holding the bookmark is a gold sunflower pendant on a chain. It's the first piece of jewelry he's ever given me. Tucked away in a book. My eyes snap up to meet his, and the love emanating from him nearly brings me to tears. While neither of us has spoken those three little words, we both know it's there. Like the joy in the air one feels during Christmas, voices as carols are sung but otherwise taken for granted. That feeling is simply there.

How am I supposed to not hug him 'til later?

"Your gift is under the tree." I point beside him to the rectangular gift box wrapped in bold blue and silver gift wrap.

He gives me a sweet grin and reaches for the package. It's not worth much. I don't make a lot working part-time at the flower shop. Yet, honestly, I love that my family doesn't do over-the-top gifts for the holidays. *Well, except that cruise.* The gifts are usually more personalized. Meaningful. Okay, maybe the ones between Alex and Ricky, not so much.

As Alex peels back the paper, he beams. I was able to

catch a great shot of him and Ricky laughing together along the railing of the cruise ship. I know Ricky moving away is going to hit him hard, and it seemed like the perfect gift.

"Sunny T." His voice sounds breathy. "This is perfect."

Ricky leans over and grins. "Hey, I want one of these."

"If you stop playing with the wooden puzzle we gave you, you might get to the other gifts still sitting under the tree." Mom laughs.

"I think there's five dollars in here," Ricky tosses back, his tongue sticking out of the corner of his mouth as he continues to try and solve the puzzle that will unlock the box.

Alex stands and comes over to where I'm sitting. "Thank you." He wraps his strong arms around me, and I have to try not to swoon in front of my entire family. God, I've missed him. And he feels and smells so good.

"You're welcome," I say as he withdraws from me. Our eyes are having a conversation we can't put words to in our present environment.

"Three more days," he mouths. Three more days until we can spend a quiet evening alone.

Chapter 20

Alex

It's the start of a new year, and I'm itching to drive to Norfolk and tell Ricky I'm dating his sister. Don't get me wrong, I'm dreading the conversation. But I'm tired of hiding how I feel about her. I want to be able to enjoy taking her out—live life like a normal couple.

We'd already missed out on New Year's Eve together. There were the usual parties, but we didn't want to be spotted out and about until we broke the news to her brother. Add to that, I had to work on New Year's Eve, and it made ringing in the New Year with Tuesday difficult. We settled for kiss emojis sent to each other at midnight.

But as my girl is a glass-half-full kinda woman, I came home at the end of my twenty-four-hour shift to find her waiting for me in my apartment. We started the year off right with breakfast, sex, a nap, black-eyed peas and stewed tomatoes for good luck, sex, football bowl games, and another nap. Undercover relationship or not, I wouldn't mind spending every New Year's Day this way.

Tuesday

There's an inch of black ice on the ground, and the 911 calls had been coming in back-to-back. Volunteering during inclement weather is no joke. The only good thing is knowing there is always the possibility of getting dispatched on a call in Alex's jurisdiction. The thrill of seeing him in his uniform on scene never gets old.

I'd just turned on the television when the loud overhead blare of an impending call rang throughout the building.

"Okay, I blame Tuesday for that. It's like you were tempting the gods, thinking you were going to have time to turn on the TV." Max laughs.

"You're probably right."

We all head to the ambulance as we listen for them to repeat the address of the 911 call as well as the details of what we're responding to.

"Medic 7, medic 7. Respond code three to an MVA on Highway 301 South at Route 54."

"Big surprise, a motor vehicle accident," Henry says as we head to the ambulance. He jumps into the driver's seat, and Max is the senior EMT, so he takes the front passenger seat while I ride in the back. If I was more invested in a medical career, I would've completed my advanced life support or paramedic training as Ricky had. But I just haven't felt motivated to add that to my already heavy course load, work, and newfound social life.

We speed down the two-lane highway, lights and sirens blazing, until we arrive on the scene of a multi-vehicle accident. It's early evening but dark, given it's January. Henry pulls up behind the last car on the shoulder and puts the ambulance in park. Grabbing the medic bag containing most of the things I'll need to stabilize a patient in a minor accident, I fling it over my shoulder and jump out the back doors of the unit.

As I come around the ambulance, my boots slide beneath me despite their tread. The ground is very slick. I wish the cars traveling near us would move over, leaving a lane clear like they're supposed to. Attempting to stick close to the vehicles in case I need something to grab onto, I walk carefully toward where the firefighters are standing. They arrive on scene first and can usually direct us on where we need to go. Coming closer, I notice one is standing facing me, a large smile evident despite the darkness that surrounds us.

My heart warms, helping to thaw my body from the frigid temperature better than any insulated squad jacket could. Deciding I'll get the update on where I can best help from him instead of Henry, I keep my sights trained on Alex until his facial expression changes.

"Tuessssssss!"

On instinct, I look over my shoulder just before everything goes black.

Chapter 21

Alex

Making the phone call to Sybil and Scott about their daughter's accident is one of the hardest things I've ever had to do. Topped only by seeing Tuesday mowed down by that car. Running to her lifeless body, I wept when I found a pulse.

Henry allowed me to jump in the unit with Max. I don't have the medical skills the paramedics possess, but there was no way I was letting her out of my sight. I should've offered to drive the ambulance, but my captain and Henry could both tell I was frantic and in no position to be driving.

We delivered her unconscious form to the medical college. It's the closest level one trauma center in the area. She was immediately whisked into the trauma bay, clothes stripped from her, and tubes placed in ungodly places. I stayed as long as I could until it was evident this wasn't a typical patient drop-off, and a nurse escorted me to the waiting room. It was there I made that fateful call to her parents before I allowed myself to fall apart.

I can't remember the last time I cried. Even when I attended my grandparent's funerals. But for all the waffling I did before I pulled my head out of my ass, it's evident now that this girl is my entire universe.

"She's got to be all right. She just has to," I mutter to myself as I pace the overcrowded room. I'm sure I look like I'm the patient and am having some type of psychotic break.

"Alex, are you staying?" Max asks, breaking me from my hysteria.

"Yes. I'm waiting for her parents to get here."

"Okay. Please tell them we're praying for her. And could you let us know how she's doing?"

"Of course."

Max pats me on the arm before heading to the ambulance to mark themselves available to take the next call. Life moving on. As if the world hadn't just ceased to exist as I knew it.

The Palmers make record time, joining me in the waiting room before heading to the triage nurse to introduce themselves and ask to speak with the emergency room attending currently providing care for Tuesday. At least they can get some intel. I likely wouldn't have gotten far stating I was her boyfriend, much less a secret boyfriend.

Fuck that. I don't care who knows anymore.

IT SEEMS LIKE I'VE BEEN SITTING OUT HERE FOREVER. THE Palmers have to come out soon and let me know something. My mind is jumping to the worst-case scenario.

As if they've heard my plea, I feel a hand on my shoulder and bolt out of my chair.

"It's okay, Alex." Tuesday's father attempts to comfort me. "They've irradiated her from stem to stern. There's no head injury that they can discern at this point. The car crushed her pelvis. They believe she lost a lot of blood. The combination of that and the trauma threw her into shock."

Falling into my seat, I run my hands through my hair. If only I'd seen that car coming sooner. If I could have run to her. "How is she? Any change?"

"No. Not yet," her mother answers, sniffling. "They took her straight to the OR. She's going to have a long road ahead of her."

My waterlogged gaze connects with her red-rimmed one, and I get the definite feeling she knows. This isn't concern for my best friend's little sister. But I don't have it in me to have that conversation right now. And if she's trying to warn me what's ahead, she's wasting her breath. My whole life is in that operating room right now. I can't even think of a world without Sunny in it.

⸺

HOURS LATER, TUESDAY'S PARENTS ARE CALLED BACK TO the recovery room to talk to the surgeon. While my mother and sisters are the praying members of our family, I take the opportunity every chance I get to plead with the man upstairs. It's in the middle of a bargaining prayer where I promise to go to church on Sundays if he'll only give Tuesday a chance, that her parents come out and advise she's been moved to the shock trauma intensive care unit or STICU for short.

"How did she look? Did everything go okay?"

Her mother looks to her father, who pulls Sybil into his side. "The surgeon said she did well. Better than expected, given the mechanism of her injury."

"But I never imagined seeing my daughter this way. She looks so frail," Sybil cries.

"You should go on home, Alex. You've had a long day."

"No," I blurt. "I... I can't."

Sybil pulls me in for a tight hug, and it's then, I'm sure. She knows. For the briefest of moments, I wonder how long they've known but dismiss it almost as soon as the thought presents itself.

"They have a family waiting area there. I'm not sure when you'll be able to see her, but at least you'll be close if that time comes."

"Thank you," I squeak out.

The three of us make our way to the STICU waiting area. We aren't there long before Scott excuses himself to check in at the nurses' station to provide his contact information and share we'll be in the waiting area. He returns to let Sybil know they've transferred Tuesday from recovery into her room, and I'm once again left to sit and wait.

Why couldn't it have been me?

———

I LOOK AT MY WATCH. IT'S ALMOST MIDNIGHT. THE Palmers went home saying they wanted to get a good night's rest to prepare for the day ahead and encouraged me to do the same. But I just can't leave her here.

I've turned this little waiting area into a makeshift motel, stripping off my boots and turnout gear. While I have no other shoes, at least I have my uniform pants and matching navy blue T-shirt with Hanover Fire's emblem imprinted on it.

Leaning my elbows on my knees, my head cradled in my hands, I try to shake the memory of my sweet Sunny smiling at me as that car skidded right into her. As much as it haunts me, I can only imagine what she'll have to contend with. Hopefully, she didn't have a chance to see it coming for her.

"Young man."

"Oh!" I jump from the seat.

"I'm so sorry. I didn't mean to startle you. I didn't realize anyone was still here until I came over to turn the lights off."

I stare blankly at her. I'm not sure how to respond without one more person trying to send me home. Hell, I can't even sleep in my car. I'd have to Uber home, and I'm. Not. Leaving. Her. Here.

"Who are you here for?"

"Tuesday." My voice cracks. "Tuesday Palmer."

The kind older nurse reaches for my hand, and I panic. Has something happened?

"Would you like to sit with her?"

"Wha? Really? I can see her?" My eyes well with tears.

"Oh, come with me." She pats my hand and tucks it into her elbow.

"Wait. I don't have any shoes."

The nurse gives me a peculiar look until I point to all of the gear I've just removed. "Ah. I'll get you some footies. It'll be all right."

She directs me to a large circular room with nurses and technicians sitting in the center, telemetry monitors beeping incessantly overhead. Across from them, the patient rooms line the perimeter. Each room with glass doors allowing easy observation of the patient resting inside.

And then I see her. The room is dim, with only a mild light shining from the monitors overhead. It creates almost a halo effect, making Tuesday look like an angel. The nurse reaches forward to slide the doors open, and a tear falls free.

"Thank you." I sniffle. "I didn't think I'd get to see her, but I couldn't—"

"There, there. What's your name?"

"I'm Alex. Alex Bell."

"It's nice to meet you, Alex Bell. I'm Gwendolyn. Things don't always go by the letter of the law on night shift." She winks. "I'll be right out there if you need anything."

I nod, trying to keep my emotions in check and move forward to sit down beside Tuesday's bed. She looks so weak and frail. But I instantly hear her optimistic voice in my head. Looks can be deceiving. Because my girl is a fighter. Anyone else might've given up on that highway. But she's still here.

Gingerly, I lift her soft hand, careful not to disrupt any of the intravenous lines or telemetry monitor wires attached to her. I just need to touch her. To somehow let her know I'm here.

"Sunny. I'm right here. I promise I won't leave. I'm sorry—" I have to halt my words to choke down a sob before continuing. "I'm sorry I couldn't get to you in time. God. I was so happy to see you. I didn't notice anything but your bright smile." Swiping my arm across my face, I try to wipe away the tears before they get her all wet. "I'm not sure if they'll let me see you tomorrow. Nurse Gwendolyn snuck me in. But I'll be in the waiting room. Don't think because I'm not beside you, I'm not here."

As much as I want her to know I'm with her, it hits me that if she can hear, I could upset her. She's been through enough. Leaning my head down by her side, I hold her hand in mine and close my eyes.

"I love you. I can't wait 'til you wake up, and I can tell you."

Chapter 22

Alex

Morning comes, and change of shift brings increased commotion outside her doors. I'm not sure what time I fell asleep, so I put my head back down, rub the pad of my thumb over Tuesday's knuckles, and close my eyes to the world around me.

A little while later, I lie unable to sleep. It's as if I'm being watched. Lifting my head to look over my shoulder, I expect to find the day shift nurse beginning her rounds until my eyes land on him.

"Ricky," I say, my mouth dry. He doesn't respond. I can't make out his expression. Is he trying to take in what's happened with his poor little sister? I'm sure his parents have filled him in.

"How long?"

"What? Has she been out? Since it happened, I think."

He nods toward our joined hands. "I meant that."

It feels so natural to hold her. I'd forgotten I was doing it. "A while."

"You're my best friend, Alex. You couldn't tell me? Two of the most important people in my life, and you were sneaking around behind my back."

"It wasn't like that. We wanted to see where things went before we brought anyone else into it. I knew you wouldn't approve of me."

"You're darn right. As best I recall, you were with Ainsley not that long ago."

"I know. I was with Ainsley because of the way I was starting to feel about your sister. I was trying to put any obstacle in the way. But I couldn't fight it anymore." I want to tell him I love her, but I'm sure as hell not sharing that with him before I can say it to Tuesday.

"What happens when you get bored and want to move on? It'll devastate her."

"That isn't going to happen." I stroke the top of her hand, hoping she can't hear any of this. "We're the real deal, man."

We're quickly interrupted as the day shift nurse comes in and advises she needs to do a few things and help clean Tuesday up a bit, but we can return later. I lift her hand to my mouth, kissing her gently before standing to head back to the waiting room.

"Nice shoes," Ricky says.

Looking down at my blue booties, I chuckle.

"You should head home and get some rest," Ricky says.

"No."

"Alex. She's safe here. I'll call you if something changes. Unless you're planning to use your body odor to wake her."

Shit. He has a point. "I can't leave her, man. You don't understand."

"Try me."

"I fought this relationship tooth and nail. Every time we would start to get close, I'd pull away. I didn't want to upset you. I didn't want to risk losing all of you if it didn't work out. I didn't want to hurt her. There was a list of excuses. But when she needed me, I wasn't there. I'm never doing that to her again."

Ricky shakes his head. "Wow. I had no idea you two were that involved. Okay. I get it. At least I appreciate you not wanting to hurt her. So long as you don't, our friendship is solid. But at least go take a shower."

"I rode here in the ambulance with her. I'd have to take an Uber home and back. That would take forever."

Ricky fishes out his keys. "I'm in the parking deck, 4th level. I'm staying at the Marriott right down the street." He hands me his key card. "Room 212."

Crushing my friend into my chest, I decide to take him up on his offer. So, hopefully, I can return as the nurses finish up. "Thank you."

"Use extra soap."

"Shut up."

———

I MAKE IT BACK TO THE STICU WAITING ROOM JUST AS A doctor is delivering an update to the Palmers. I stop in my tracks, unsure whether I should step away and give them some privacy, until Sybil waves me in.

"Dr. Knight, this is Alex. Tuesday's boyfriend."

"Nice to meet you."

"He was just letting us know that she appears to be doing well, and he suspects her remaining unconscious is likely related to the strong pain medication she's been receiving."

I let out an exhale. I hadn't thought about that.

"If things go well, she'll be moved to a step down unit in a few days where she doesn't require the immense level of one-on-one care that she does now. She'll likely be here a few weeks and then transfer to an inpatient rehab facility until she's able to go home. Given the hardware she now has in her pelvis, her recovery is likely to take three months. She won't be able to walk for six to ten weeks. She could have long-term effects that limit her function for at least a year."

"But she's here. And she's a fighter. So we've got this," I interject. I'm tired of the gloom and doom. While they've graciously covered my shifts until Tuesday is in the clear, I'm limited by my fire schedule. But I'll gladly put the towing business on hold or rent out my truck to someone so I can be Tuesday's cheerleader. I'll be there when the rehab folks have left, reminding her just how strong she is.

Sybil reaches for my arm, and I look at her.

"She's going to need all of us. Sunny T is going to be fine. I'm sure of it," I say.

As the surgeon leaves, we take turns visiting Tuesday. I plan to stay the night, so I let her family spend the majority of the day with her. As night shift comes, I greet Gwendolyn, who smiles as she comes in and out of Tuesday's room.

As I had the night before, I lay my head down and begin to drift off when I hear Gwendolyn behind me.

"Well, hello there."

My head springs up from the mattress, curious who's come to visit at this hour, when I notice there's no one but Gwendolyn there. And she's looking over my shoulder. I swivel my head toward Tuesday like a bobblehead and freeze when I see those beautiful big green eyes staring at me.

"Oh, baby. Thank God." I lower my head and try not

to weep. Suddenly, her sweet hand is in my hair, stroking the back of my head. My beautiful, brave girl is lying here, screwed back together like the Tin Man in the *Wizard of Oz*, but she awakes to comfort me.

"Are you hurting, dear?" Gwendolyn asks.

"No." Her voice comes out brittle. "I—" She immediately winces as she adjusts herself in the bed. "What happened?"

I explain the events of the last few days, surprised she doesn't remember much. I worry when it does, she may have a hard time with it. But for now, that's one less stressor. I explain what the future holds, and I can see it's overwhelming her. "You're not alone, Sunny. You've got your family, Grace, and me. We all love you. We'll do anything we can to help you through this."

It takes a minute before she stops fidgeting with her bedsheets and looks at me. "You love me?"

"God, yes. I'm so in love with you I can't see straight." I laugh. It feels good to finally tell her.

Her smile lights up the room, and I know we're going to be okay.

Chapter 23

Three months later
Alex

The months that followed were grueling. Tuesday had to put her life on hold and focus solely on getting stronger. She was in a wheelchair for months. The endless physical and occupational therapy helped her to make strides but wore her out. It was more important than ever that she knew I was by her side and would do anything and everything to help her regain her life.

The Palmers have been great about letting me spend so much time at their home. I've practically moved in. With my rotating schedule at the fire department, it only made sense for Sunny to stay in her home, where she could receive therapy, and her mother or father could assist her if I was on duty.

Yet she's come a long way, and the time has come to regain some privacy.

"Why are you so jumpy?" I ask as we sit in the waiting room of her orthopedic surgeon's office.

"I don't know. It feels like graduation day. That this visit could mark the start of so many new things after all of this time. Not needing constant supervision, getting my life back, returning to work at Cygnature Blooms—"

"Moving in with me," I interrupt.

Tuesday beams at me.

"Tuesday," the nurse calls from the doorway.

We stand and follow her down the hall to Dr. Knight's office. She ushers us inside and reassures us he will be with us shortly. Looking about the room, there are no personal photos or mementos—just various certificates and degrees on display.

All of a sudden, Dr. Knight appears and greets us before sitting down. Tuesday looks at me and smiles before reaching for my hand. Shit. I know this girl loves me. She didn't bat an eye when doctor tall, rich, and handsome walked in. Orthopedist extraordinaire Dr. Holden Knight is impressive. He's talented, good-looking, and appears pretty humble. I mean, I'm a dude, and I'd hit that.

"I wanted to start by saying how impressed I am with your tenacity, Ms. Palmer. You've endured quite a tragic accident and bounced back impressively. While you'll still likely face some obstacles, I think the worst is behind you."

"I'm glad you brought that up, Dr. Knight. It's not something I'm considering anytime soon. But I want to be clear on what the future holds."

Confused, I turn to see she's struggling to finish her statement.

"Can I still have kids?"

I get a lump in my throat. I never even considered this before. This could be devastating for her. Me too, if I'm being honest. But I'm not opposed to adoption if we need to.

"I'm glad you brought that up. It's a misconception

that most people with pelvic fractures, such as yours, cannot have children. Some may require cesarean section versus delivering vaginally, but the majority have healthy pregnancies without complication."

Tuesday visibly exhales, and I can see her shoulders relax. I didn't realize how much this had been weighing on her.

"The other area I would encourage you to feel free to discuss with me is intercourse."

What the fuck? I drop Tuesday's hand as both of mine ball into fists. Okay, maybe I'll be hitting him in a different way.

He must notice my face reddening and interjects, "This is an area many find embarrassing to discuss with their doctor. And unfortunately, I suspect many of my colleagues may prefer to avoid the discussion altogether. Yet it's important. This can obviously affect your quality of life. Some patients, men and women, can struggle with inter-course following a fracture like yours. Only time will tell. But it's not uncommon for patients to have long term struggles. If this becomes an issue for you, please let me know. There are pelvic floor exercises that can be performed with physical therapy, biofeedback, lots of options. I don't want you to suffer in silence."

I sit dumbfounded. I never considered this either. Purely focused on her recovery, it never dawned on me this could be a problem down the road. But it's not surprising. I'm glad he was so forthright about it. *This fucker really is smooth.*

———

HAVING LEFT DR. KNIGHT'S OFFICE WITH A LITTLE MORE spring in her step, we decide to grab lunch before returning home.

"Do you feel good about how things went?"

"Yes." She nods over her turkey club.

"I hadn't thought about the impact this could have on our sex life," I admit.

"Me either. I only worried about carrying a baby to term with hardware holding my pelvis together. I never considered sex could be a problem."

"I need you to be honest when the time comes. Please don't shut me out if you're in pain or having any issues. I want to know what you're feeling."

She reaches out to squeeze my hand. "I have a good feeling about us. I think we'll find a way to overcome whatever life throws at us."

Lifting her hand to my mouth, I kiss the inside of her palm. This food has nothing on my sweet girl.

"Oh. Did I ever tell you I met a girl in North Carolina after your birthday cruise?"

Tuesday sits up straighter in her chair, pulls her sandwich from her mouth, and gives me the worst glare I've ever seen. "I wondered what happened when you ghosted me. Now I'm not sure I want to know."

"What? No. No. That came out all wrong. I went to Sycamore Mountain with some friends to clear my head. And while I was there, I met a girl who designs gourmet cakes and cupcakes. She was saying how she wanted to expand her little shop and join forces with a creative florist to bring a unique vision to the clients who order from her for garden parties, weddings, and the like. I told her you'd be perfect for the job."

Tuesday's face lights up like nothing I've ever seen. It's probably the most luminous I've seen her since the accident. "I'd love to meet her. It sounds amazing."

"Well, why don't we plan a trip? Sycamore Mountain,

here we come."

Tuesday

"Oh, Tuesday. I'm so proud of you. You've done so well with rehab, and now my baby girl is moving out on her own," Mom says.

I smile. I'm grateful she and Dad have been so accepting of my decision to move in with Alex.

"Just don't let your living situation distract you from your studies."

"About that." I wince as I try to find the right words. "I'd like to finish my degree. But I don't want to be a nurse."

My mother looks at me with a flat affect.

"I know how important it is to you to have Ricky and me follow in your footsteps. But I'm not interested in health care. At all. I didn't mind volunteering, but not enough to do it for a living. If that accident taught me nothing else, it's to seize the day."

"Honey, I'm just surprised. I had no idea you didn't want to be a nurse."

"I want to have my own floral shop one day. I'm at peace when I'm at Cygnature Blooms, surrounded by flowers. The few days a month I work there are some of the happiest I have. I want to work at a job I love. Not one I tolerate."

"You're absolutely right. Working your whole life is hard enough. You should follow your passion. And if your passion is flowers, then so be it."

I wrap my arms around my mother, squeezing her tight. "You have no idea how relieved I am."

"Oh, honey. We love you. We only want to see you happy."

Pulling back from her, I stop to reflect on all the positives in my life. Alex and I have been looking online at Sycamore Mountain, and we're excited to visit and meet Addison at her bake shop. He even said he'd be willing to consider a transfer there if working with her became a serious possibility. I just can't believe it.

While some would focus on how my life has turned upside down following the accident, I choose to see it differently. I've faced adversity head-on and won. I have an amazing supportive family. I'm going to pursue my dream job. And I'm in love with my brother's best friend.

How can things get any better than this?

Want more? Click here for a bonus scene with Alex and Tuesday

Alex makes his first appearance in ***Moonshot***

You can read more about Addison and Trevor in Naughty & Nice

You can read more about Gavin in the fall of 2023 in Dr. Weston (as well as in The Deprivation Trilogy and The Bitter Rival duet.)

And to grab the other books in the Wild Blooms series, keep reading to the end of this book.

Keep turning for a sneak peek from The Bitter Rival.

The Bitter Rival
(SNEAK PEEK)

"Uh, Bella? Why on earth would you come back here with me when you could keep dancing with tall, dark, and *fuck me, is he sexy*? Jeez, he's the hottest man I think I've ever seen. I almost had an orgasm watching him move his hands all over you. That look on his face. Gah," she utters, fanning herself.

I can't possibly find an answer that will appease her, so I simply shrug my shoulders.

She gives me a blank stare, mimicking my ridiculous motion by drawing her shoulders up toward her ears in question. "What is wrong with you? That man is beautiful."

"Yeah, a little too beautiful."

"Huh?"

"The way he was looking at me, Bailey, and touching me... I was starting to feel like shark bait," I reply as I swiftly look toward the bar for a waiter. I need another drink.

"Well, hell, Bella. I'd let him bite me," she scolds, waggling her brows in my direction.

"Bailes, something tells me if a guy like that takes a bite out of you, you won't recover."

CLICK HERE TO KEEP READING

Acknowledgments

I cannot thank TL Swan enough for starting me on this journey. This dream would have remained locked in my soul had it not been for her.

Thank you to my incredible team. Kelly and Cheree continue to put the finishing touches on my work, and Logan with Bearded Goat Books stepped up to do my formatting. Thank you to Sarah at The Book Cover Boutique for designing this beauty, and to Kate at Kate Decided to Design for creating my discrete paperback. Thank you to Stephanie, for all the behind the scenes work you do. To Brittni for always being there when I need her. And lastly to Give Me Books who ensure readers find my work.

I'd never make it to the editing stage without the help of my alpha and beta readers. Denise, Siri, Susan, Rita, Kelly, Emma, Erica, and Kate. You're such a gift. Thank you!

To my ARC readers, book bloggers, and social media followers. I love you all so much. I'm so incredibly appreciative for all you continue to do for me.

And I'm most grateful to my family who have supported me as I try to accomplish my dream.

About the Author

Born and raised in Virginia, LM Fox currently lives in a suburb of Richmond with her husband, three kids, and a chocolate lab.

Her pastimes are traveling to new and favorite places, trying new foods, a swoony book with either a good cup of tea or coffee, margaritas on special occasions, and watching her kids participate in a variety of sports.

She has spent the majority of her adult life working in emergency medicine, and her books are written in this setting. Her main characters are typically in the medical field, EMS, fire, and/or law enforcement. She enjoys writing angsty, contemporary romance starring headstrong, independent heroines you can't help but love and the hot alpha men who fall hard for them.

Join LM Fox in her group on Facebook by CLICKING HERE!!

Also by LM Fox

The Deprivation Trilogy
DEPRIVATION
FRACTURED
STRONGER
DEPRIVED NO MORE, THE EPILOGUE

New Releases
MR. SECOND BEST
MOONSHOT (An interconnected prequel to The
Deprivation Trilogy)

Sycamore Series
NAUGHTY AND NICE, A Complete Standalone

Steamy Reads
THE BITTER RIVAL
SWEET SURRENDER, THE EPILOGUE

Wild Bloom Series

Complete WILD BLOOMS Series

Don't forget to leave a review for your favorite books.

Snapdragons and Seductions - Sofia Aves
Saffron and Secrets - Sharon Woods
Blossom and Bliss - L.A. Shaw
Willows and Waterlilies - Taylor K Scott
Roses and Redemption - Denise T Ford
Wildflowers and Whispers - Maci Dillon
Bluebonnets and Bikers - D. Lilac
Magnolias and Memories - T M Caruso
Lavender and Lust - Jaclyn Combe

Jasmine and Jealousy - Rhiannon Marina
Tulips and Truths - Mila Chase
Lilacs and Lovers - J R Gale
Chrysanthemum and Smolder - V L Peters
Lotus and Longing - LaLa Montgomery
Daisies and Desire - Ann Penny
Sunflowers and Surrender - L M Fox
Forget-me-nots and Fireworks - Elle Nicoll
Peonies and Promises - Lizzie Moreton
Heather and Heartache - VR Tennent

All books are available in e-book and paperback.

Printed in Great Britain
by Amazon

26051288R00081